Break Heart Canyon

by

Gini Rifkin

Break Heart Canyon

Cover Art by *The Wild Rose Press, Inc.*

The Wild Rose Press, Inc.
PO Box 708
Adams Basin, NY 14410-0708
Visit us at www.thewildrosepress.com

Publishing History
First Edition, 2022
Trade Paperback ISBN 978-1-5092-4458-4
Digital ISBN 978-1-5092-4459-1

Published in the United States of America

Ryker believed this woman was capable of casting a spell on him. She needn't bother, he was already smitten. Yes, smitten. Never in his life had that term seemed relevant. The rampage of feelings she stirred in him ran the gambit from wanting to bed her, to wanting to protect her, to wanting to walk away from her as fast as possible.

She was a danger to his way of life. Or maybe his way of life was a danger to his happiness. Una confused him. Made him unsettled. And what a fetching picture she created, one easy to commit to memory and long for at a later date. But he wasn't fond of wasting time on lonely reflections—he needed to vacate the cabin.

"Anything I can do for you other than get out of your way?"

"More firewood is always appreciated."

He hurried outside, relieved to have a legitimate reason for performing any activity other than standing and staring at her like a randy schoolboy. Returning with all the split wood he could carry, he deposited the armload by the stove and turned to leave.

"Thank you, Ryker."

For the first time, she'd called him by his Christian name, and dang he liked the sound of it wrapped in her unpredictable Scottish burr.

"You're welcome, Una." His reply came over his shoulder as he left. The jaunty tune she hummed hesitated for a moment. He smiled. Did she like the sound of her name on his lips as well?

Dedication

For Norma, an extraordinary woman,
loved by many and greatly missed.
Your memory lives on in our hearts.

Author's Note

In 1878 America, the western frontier was exciting, dangerous, and everchanging. The Transcontinental Railroad was up and running, the Pinkerton Agency was chasing Jesse James, and the single action Colt revolver was on the hip of most men who carried a pistol. There was a real Long Branch Saloon in Dodge City, Bat Masterson was 25 years old, and Stanley had found Livingstone.

With the discovery of dinosaur artifacts in Como Bluff, Wyoming and Garden Park, Colorado, the Bone Wars had also begun. In a race to obtain the highly sought-after ancient relics, confrontations arose that were as underhanded and dangerous as any skirmish fought with a long rifle and cannon. Ryker Landry's thirst for adventure landed him in the middle of such turmoil. But he didn't plan on getting caught in the crossfire—or losing his heart to a Scottish lass, as bold and fiery as her long red hair.

Chapter One

July, 1878, near Cañon City, Colorado

"Come oot right now. Are you hearin' me?"

Ryker Landry kept to the shadows. The voice ordering him out of the cave was female—one with a bit of a Scottish brogue. Maybe if he remained silent, calling her bluff, she'd go away.

"I said come oot. I ken you're in there."

So much for that idea.

"You got three shakes of a billy goat's tail to decide. Then I'm a sendin' in MacTavish."

MacTavish? The image of a brawny Scotsman wrapped in a kilt and a nasty disposition took form in Ryker's mind. He wasn't in the mood today for a fight. Besides, other than a little trespassing, he hadn't done anything wrong—yet.

Seeing no other option, he eased from the darkness of the cave into the daylight, squinting as the glare of the sun hit him full force.

The female pointing a battered Winchester rifle at his chest stepped back, keeping a safe distance between them. Caught by the breeze, her hair fluttered and curled like a handful of ginger-colored ribbons. The no-nonsense glare in her eyes, as green as the grass upon which she stood, held him in place.

He glanced around for the person she'd called

MacTavish, but saw no one other than her dog. So far, the fearsome creature kept to her side—a deerhound by the looks of him. Ryker had seen such animals in the Highlands of Scotland.

"Good morning, madam." Ryker doffed his hat and showered her with his most radiant smile. The woman didn't respond to either affectation.

"Dinnae good morning me. Besides, it's after the noon hour. You need to get off me property, and don't be lookin' back." As if on cue, the dog growled, emphasizing the woman's stern words. "Be still, MacTavish, he's leaving."

So MacTavish was the dog. A dubious relief. He'd rather tangle with a man than this beast.

"Before I take my leave, might I know by whom I'm being held at gunpoint."

"Ma name's Una MacLaren, and this is my land." She raised her chin in a stubborn tilt as if she challenged the whole world with her words, not just him.

Inclined to beg forgiveness, rather than ask for permission, Ryker saw he had little choice but to admit to his indiscretion of trespass. "Pleased to make your acquaintance. I'm Ryker Landry, on expedition in search of dinosaur artifacts. I meant no harm. There are rumors unusual specimens can be found in the surrounding canyon, especially this cave." He nodded over his shoulder. He'd been searching out in the west for several hot dusty weeks. This was the closest he'd come to tracking down the item he'd been paid to find.

"So, you decided to just come trapsin' in here and help yourself?" Outrage seemed to resonate through her body, setting the fringe on her plaid shawl quaking.

"I was merely taking a gander around. I'll gladly pay a decent price for anything I find."

"You can't put a price on hallowed items. And to the ancient people of this land, those bones and relics are sacred. I'm inclined to think they should be staying right where they are—undisturbed. Next thing you'll be setting loose the spunkies and wulvers, or bringin' the curse of the canyon down upon us."

The curse of the what? She seemed serious. He hadn't recalled any legend about the canyon being haunted. And what in tarnation were those other things she mentioned? Was she trying to scare him off? Although, come to think of it, he had experienced a sudden chill while in the cave—along with the distinct feeling he wasn't alone. He'd attributed both sensations to the high altitude found in Colorado. Upon his arrival, he'd gotten dizzy on a few occasions.

Remaining silent, he considered this Scottish lass who appeared to believe in legends and myths. How could he use her superstitious nature to his advantage? "A curse you say. Even more fascinating. I can well imagine the unusual abounds in this dark canyon. I'm willing to pay for information about the surrounding area as well as about the artifacts." By all appearances, especially the state of the tattered barn roof, her finances were lacking. Would she take the bait for the money she appeared to need?

"We don't want your coinage, Mr. Landry." The beast of a hound growled menacingly. "MacTavish is getting annoyed, so you'd best take your leave as asked."

"Yes, of course. Wouldn't want to upset your dog" Unless staring at his mistress whom he seemed to adore, the animal had malice in his fearsome golden eyes. "Nice to have met you, Una MacLaren, I'll just mosey along then."

Never lowering the rifle, she encouraged his departure. "My property ends a good way beyond the creek. Keep moseying until you reach there."

He couldn't resist one more try at gaining access to her land. "Please consider my offer. Perhaps we could meet again at your convenience, and you can enlighten me regarding the folklore around here."

"Have ya cornflowers in your ears? I said get out and dinnae come back."

Retreat sounding the better part of valor, Ryker grabbed the knapsack he'd left by the cave entrance and followed her instructions. The hound barked and snapped at the air, encouraging him to step lively.

****

Una lowered the rifle but stood guard until the man splashed his way across Strawberry Creek and then disappeared into the woods. Sucking in a big breath, she exhaled slowly, and her shoulders sagged in relief. What next? Bad enough she had to defend her land from the underhanded cattlemen, now this hooligan turns up.

He certainly seemed full of himself, bold as brass wandering on her land. The offer of money and a fetching smile wouldn't have her going against her principles.

Grabbing a handful of skirt in her free hand, she raised the hem and stomped through the underbrush, heading back up the small hill toward her barn and cabin.

"MacTavish, you behaved well. I could tell you

wanted a piece of that scallywag, but you held back. I know you wid nae hae gone in the cave after him, but he had no idea and our bluff worked. Leading me here in the first place to find the intruder was bonny good work, too. I'm proud of ye."

Reveling in her praise, the deerhound leaped joyfully at her side, and she laughed at his antics. What would she do without MacTavish?

"Come along now. No time for play. We're late with chores. Blossom appeared unwell earlier today, as does the kid she birthed a few weeks ago. She could use a little extra love and attention." *Who couldn't?*

As she walked, Una rotated her shoulders easing the knotted-up muscles in her back. Sometimes there didn't seem enough hours in the day for all the work needing to be done. Other times, especially when she was sorely missing Hamish, the lonely hours seemed to stretch into forever.

****

Retreating to the nearby woods, Ryker stood in the small clearing beside the firepit he'd dug the night before. Peering through the trees, he caught a glimpse of the woman as she walked away. Ever vigilant, the dog ran at her side. Both promised to be trouble for him. How was he going to gain her trust, or trick her into relinquishing the valuable artifact he suspected lay hidden in the cave?

The Great Dinosaur Rush was on, and fossil hunting in Colorado and Wyoming was big business. Both Yale and the Academy of Natural Sciences were financing expeditions. And two well-known paleontologists, Othniel Charles Marsh, and Edward Drinker Cope, fought ruthlessly for the best specimens.

The men sought fame and glory and government funding, and the Bone Wars had become a true battle, no holds barred.

Of course, fine examples existed in curio shops back East, much more convenient for purchase. But his employer, Mr. Cockrell, wanted one specific unique item. The crowning glory to complete his personal collection, something to brag about and lord over those in his high society circle of friends. Regardless of cost or consequences, the man aimed to have his way.

Poking a stick at the dead coals in the firepit, Ryker decided against rekindling a fire and settled on jerky and hardtack for lunch. As he ate, he considered his next move.

Before his departure for the Wild West, Ryker had been supplied with printed articles and instructions regarding the supposed location of the ancient warrior breastplate decorated with dinosaur teeth. And he was betting the relic awaited him in that cave—unless someone had gotten there first.

Mr. Cockrell refused to say how he'd heard about the myth. Apparently, private purveyors of unusual objects had their own unique underground message system. From Bombay to the Australian Outback to London and then New York, bizarre information circled the globe. The recipients of said communications were generally folks with an obsession for the unusual, and with more money than they knew what to do with.

He paced beside the firepit, and stared back toward the creek. Crossing paths with that stubborn female, was going to make his job harder—but not impossible. Maybe more interesting too.

All he needed to know was Cockrell was willing to

pay for retrieval, and he was willing to do whatever was necessary to make that happen.

Chapter Two

Una adjusted the bridle and tightened the crupper. Then she eased the cart forward, aligning the shafts on each side of Wallace, her donkey. Threading the wooden poles through the loops on the back saddle, she attached the traces, and double checked the girth.

They were almost ready to head for town.

"Just a moment longer, Wallace. You're such a good boy." She stroked the donkey's ears, his favorite pleasure. His mouth relaxed, his bottom lip drooping and trembling in delight. She should put on his blinders, but he enjoyed their outings too. They both liked glancing about to see what changes had been wrought by Nature and Man since the last time they'd ventured out.

Loosely hitching Wallace to a rail, she herded Lolly the goose, the ducks, and the chickens into their covered shelter. She didn't like leaving them out when she was gone—even if MacTavish was on guard duty. Bobcats, hawks, and Wily the fox, were as sneaky and underhanded as the cattlemen who prowled the area. Man, or beast, they were all intent on doing as much damage as possible to her and her land.

"I won't be gone long, laddie." MacTavish whined at being separated from her, and the feeling cut both ways. She felt safer with him at her side, but when choosing between the protection of the land or her, the land usually won.

Securing the tie on her wide brimmed hat, she unhitched Wallace, climbed into the two wheeled cart, and clucked the donkey into action.

They moved along at a gentle pace, her gaze wandering across the valley. Her valley, lush and green after the spring rains and dotted with the wooly white goats she loved. Just the sight of her little herd grazing peacefully eased her heart and soul.

But there were times when things weren't so pretty, like the winter they'd just survived. The valley had been filled with three feet of snow, and she thought the huge mounds would never melt. And then there was the summer two years ago, when they barely got any rain. The valley had been parched and brown, tumbleweeds the best crop.

At times, life here was nearly as hard as back home in Scotland. She missed her homeland, but her family was gone, reduced only to memories. Nothing waited for her there.

Brave and courageous, Hamish, her husband had come to America first. He worked the land for two years, building the house and establishing their flock of goats. Being away from Hamish had been hard. They hadn't been married long, but he wanted a better life for the two of them. Times were tough in the old country, and they only got worse when Great Britain began importing wool from America.

Settling here had been a good plan, one she imagined they would face and enjoy together. Now Hamish was gone too, leaving her to fend for herself, and she prayed she could keep the farm afloat without him.

The repetitive clip-clop, clip-clop of Wallace's hooves lulled her thoughts down a happier path, and settling back in the seat she grinned at the bright pink wheels of her cart. After purchasing the used conveyance, Hamish had meticulously repaired the worn leather seat and repainted her little *carriage*. The day she'd arrived she'd been overjoyed to find the conveyance waiting for her.

Hamish confessed he'd intended the wheels and sides to be dark red and not pink, but he'd added an abundance of milk and not enough rust in the paint mixture. She loved the jaunty color, but he refused to be seen riding in the *girly wagon*, which always made her laugh.

There were happy memories like this one too, she must not lose track of those.

When a large hare bolted across the road, Wallace stopped short, bringing the cart to an immediate halt. Una jerked back against the seat and held tight to the reins in case he panicked and ran. A sensible little beast, rather than shying or leaping about like a horse might do, Wallace studied the situation and then valiant as his name, he continued on. She'd named him after William Wallace, the Scottish hero and freedom fighter of her homeland. Fighting for freedom was close to many a Scot's heart.

How she'd come to own Wallace was more the donkey's idea than hers. Their horse tragically colic'd and died and Hamish soon followed falling to his death in the canyon. This left Una in dire straits with no way to get to town and no one to help around the farm. She saved every penny possible, but a horse cost more money than she had, and she must save some out for shearing season.

Then one bright spring day, a donkey turned up in her yard. He was actually peeking in the kitchen window and had scared her half to death. The poor beast's hair was worn away on his back and sides. Most likely from carrying heavy loads on maladjusted pack frames, and his hooves were sorely in need of a farrier's attention.

The farmer who owned the donkey tracked him to her farm and began beating him for running away. She'd grabbed the whip from the man, and with MacTavish to back her up, the wretched farmer soon lost his bluster.

After a heated negotiation, the man agreed to sell Wallace for five dollars. The price, less than that for a horse, was still too much. But there was no way Una would let this sweet-faced animal remain in the hands of that horrid man.

She never regretted the transaction. Wallace was an easy keeper, a hard worker, and good company. She should make inquiries and find a lady donkey for Wallace. He shouldn't live alone just because she did.

As the town of Cañon City came into view, Wallace picked up the pace. He liked visiting in town. Being a rather handsome lad, and with the colorful woolen strips braided and woven in his bridle, the children usually stopped to say hello and tickle his ears. The horses and cattlemen in town were less receptive, both of which she steered clear of if possible.

Reaching the outskirts of the city, they crossed the Arkansas River without incident, not always the case if the water was running high. Then they quickly scooted under the Denver and Rio Grande Railroad trestle.

Wallace was not a fan of the noisy smoke snorting monster that ran on the tracks, and neither was she. There was no getting him near the rails if they hummed with an approaching a train, or if one had just passed. Today they proceeded with ease.

The town was busy, and she fell in behind a dray hauling beer to the saloon. Big and slow, the conveyance cut a good swath for them to follow. Business was brisk at the Fremont Bank, and several people were gathered and chatting outside Agard's Hardware and Stoves.

When they reached Main Street, the dray turned right, and Una turned left. For a small town, Una marveled at the abundance of churches represented—Episcopal, Presbyterian, Baptist, Methodist, and Roman Catholic. All within blocks of one another, all living in relative peace. For centuries, religious upheaval had wounded and scarred her beloved Scotland, another incentive for many to leave. In America, the way of thinking about many things was different, more accepting—at least on the surface. Some hearts continued to carry bad intentions and not everyone was treated equally.

Turning onto Mill Road, she followed the street to Third, and finally to the schoolhouse. Being summer, there wouldn't be any children there today, but she figured her friend Kathleen would be around. The only schoolteacher, Kathleen or Kate, could be found most days attending to repairs or preparing lessons for the coming fall. The woman never seemed to rest.

Una maneuvered the cart close to the front door and scrambled to the ground. Attaching a long lead to Wallace's bridle, she let him graze on the plentiful grass.

"Kathleen, are ye aboot, my friend?" Ugh, she forgot to tone down her Scottish accent. Although Kathleen wouldn't care, when around other people, Una tried to blend in more and keep to herself the fact she was an immigrant with funny sounding speech and a propensity for the old ways. Yet, try as she might, if scared or excited there was no stopping the brogue coming out at will.

"Kate, are you here?"

Entering the wooden structure, Una found her friend sitting in a chair and fanning herself with a sheaf of paper.

"What's this? I didn't expect to find you a lollygagging around. Why is your face so flushed?" The day wasn't exceptionally warm, was her friend ill? "Are you unwell?" She hadn't seen her friend for many months and as she drew closer, Kate's condition became apparent.

"Oh, gracious. Look at you. You've a bairn on the way. And you didnae say a word."

Kate nodded. "I needed to be sure. I've lost a babe before, and I wanted to keep this one secret for a while longer. These warm days wear me out quickly though."

"Here." Una retrieved a cup sitting nearby and handed the water to her friend.

"Thank you." Kate drank thirstily. "As I tried to re-attach the window covering on the east wall, the sun got the better of me."

"The older lads in the school should be helping ye with such tasks," Una gained her feet and repaired the sagging cloth shade.

"A good measure of the children come from the

surrounding farms. They've plenty of chores at home and soon they'll be planting seedlings for winter wheat. They already brought over and chopped enough wood for the coming year, so I dare not complain."

"I'm glad you're assured of being warm. According to the goat's fleece there could be a hard winter ahead of us." Una didn't want to imagine having to survive another bad winter.

Kate set the cup aside. "Walking from my house to the school, I noticed several cattlemen in town. You'd best be careful around here today."

The high and mighty cattlemen in the area were nothing but trouble. They hated fences, goats, sheep, and basically anyone who got in their way. When her husband died and she refused to sell out to them, their animosity hung in the air like the stench wafting off a carrion pile.

"Thank you for the warning, I'll watch for them. What else might I be doing for you before I'm down the road?"

"Nothing, truly. I've only a bit of paperwork to be sorted out and then I'm for home. Jordie promised if the weather held, he'd take me for a ride in the country. He's been so attentive to my condition. What a wonderful husband I have." She grasped and held one of Una's hands. "Oh dear, I'm sorry to go on and on about Jordie when…"

"Don't be concerned. I'm happy for you and want to share your joy. My sorrow remains great, and still comes easily and stays too long, but I adore hearing about you and Jordie. And now your plans for the wean.

"Thank you. You're my best friend, and I wish I could see you more often. And who knows what the future holds for you." Kate gave the hand she held a little squeeze of encouragement. "You're too pretty and too precious to stay single for long."

Una slid her hand free. "Kate, your optimism knows no bounds." She didn't want to be alone, but to love another man seemed impossible. When Hamish died falling off a rocky ledge, it felt as if a giant hand had squeezed all the love from her heart, reducing the organ to a lump of muscle and sinew with only one purpose—keep beating until God decided otherwise.

"Well, just keep an open mind and heart," Kate gently advised. Resigned to her situation, Una clung to the bits of tattered happiness created by the beauty of the farm and the antics of the animals. And for now, this contentment sustained her.

"I promise. Why just this morning, I found a man on my property. Too bad I had to run him off at gunpoint." Now she could laugh at the memory, but at the time she'd been frightened.

"Good gracious. Did he mean to do you harm?"

"I don't believe so. He was searching for artifacts, poking around inside the Spirit Cave on my property. Since the discovery of dinosaur bones near Cañon City there are fossil hunters scrambling willy-nilly all through the canyons and foothills. The Bone Wars have come to our own backyard."

"Why Jordie said the same thing. The other day a fierce fellow came into the bank asking for a safe deposit box. Jordie has just been promoted to keeping charge of the security services." Kate's eyes sparkled and noticeable pride filled her voice. "He was surprised when the man deposited bones, not money. Who would imagine skeletons of animals dead for thousands of years would be worth such a fuss and command so great a price back East?"

"Did Jordie describe the man?"

"Yes. A rugged, no nonsense, individual. And while short on words and manners, he was long on black hair and a menacing expression. He carried a rifle and had a revolver strapped to his hip."

Why was she so happy the description didn't fit her interloper?

****

Having been found on the MacLaren property, and tired of living rough, Ryker had decided to let a room in town. The older he became, the harder soldier-of-fortuning got. When he slept several nights on the ground, his thigh took to aching from an old bullet wound, and his back twitched where the sharp tip of Spanish Federales' saber had found him.

Now, eating his lunch at a back table in the hotel restaurant, he observed the other patrons and enjoyed the feeling he'd made a tiny bit of progress. He was sure he'd found the correct cave. Located near what the locals called Break Heart Canyon, this had to be the one.

The other signs marked on his map were present too. If you stood at the entrance to the canyon and faced due east, you could see Cougar Rock, a stony outcropping resembling a lunging mountain lion. And venturing farther between the towering walls of rock, he'd found the overgrown grotto. Without the chart, he never would have noticed the mysterious altar-like pile of stone.

Too bad nobody in town had mentioned the land was owned by a redheaded firebrand of a woman.

Hoping to avoid another confrontation with the obstinate lady and her fearsome dog, he decided to work during the night and sleep during the day. Always dark inside the cave, what time he chose to investigate the airless depths hardly mattered.

After a coffee refill, Ryker slid the plates off to the side and re-examined the packet of information he'd brought down from his room.

Before he'd set out on this venture, Ryker had been supplied by Mr. Cockrell with a leather pouch containing maps, pictures, and printed documents. The information covered details of landmarks, and particulars about the relic. The route on how to get here had been more hit and miss. Fortunately, he'd acquired updated information when he passed through Kansas City. Had he not done so, he would still be wandering around three hundred miles to the north.

From Kansas City, he and his horse headed south via the Denver and Rio Grande Railroad, which delivered them here, to the doorstep of Cañon City.

Enroute, he passed by the intriguing Castle Rock, and remarkable Pikes Peak—twelve hundred square feet of granite bursting fourteen thousand feet into the air. You didn't see mountains like that east of the Mississippi. With the coming of the solar eclipse, people were already vying for space at the summit. The spectacle would be easily seen in several parts of Colorado. Cañon City was even abuzz with tourists and amateur astronomers.

Slipping a booklet from the pouch, he glanced again at the general information, and had to admit, these prehistoric creatures and the bones they left behind were a fascination. The dinosaur teeth decorating the relic he sought commanded a high price. They came from a creature call a stega-something. Where was that? He shuffled through more papers but couldn't put his fingers on the passage. Hairpipes, feathers, and quills made up the rest of the ancient breastplate.

To unearth the teeth to create the sacred ornament must have taken generations of shamans. After decades of praying and chanting, think of the life force contained in the artifact. And with what power would the ceremonial object imbue the wearer—if you believed in that sort of thing.

Returning the parchment to the leather pouch, and then laying his money down for the meal plus a tip for Polly, the cute waitress, Ryker left the restaurant.

As he ambled down the boardwalk, the afternoon breeze turned serious, and Ryker settled his hat more securely. He'd be sad to lose the headgear. He'd picked up the wide brimmed hat years ago in Australia, and like a journal, the tattered edges recorded the adventures he'd enjoyed through the years.

Deciding he needed another kerosine lantern, he stopped at the mercantile/hardware store. Wouldn't hurt to get few boxes of Lucifers while there. He had flint and steel, of course, but those darn manufactured matches sure came in handy.

Outside the store, he paused to stare at a donkey and cart tethered to the hitching rail. Those were the brightest pink wheels and sideboards he'd ever seen on a conveyance. Still wondering who would drive such a whimsical eyesore, he went inside.

Maneuvering around several cowhands as they milled about the entrance, he headed for the back of the store and the shelf of lanterns. On the way, he grabbed a shovel and pickax. They'd be mighty useful too.

The men seemed a rowdy bunch, and more than one smelled like he'd already been partaking freely down at the saloon. As Ryker perused the items available, a mass of silky red hair caught his attention. He peeked through the shelving. Yep, it was her, one aisle over. His back went stiff, and he glanced around for her beast of a dog. Not seeing the critter, he relaxed. Keeping out of sight, he circled around to the back of the store again as she headed for the cash register.

"Well, lookie here, boys. If it ain't Miss Sheep Dip herself. Ready to sell yet?"

The men blocked Una MacLaren's path, but she stood her ground, refusing to retreat. "My animals are goats not sheep, you big bully."

At her retort, Ryker couldn't suppress a smile.

"Still smell the same to a cattleman."

"I'm sure you smell the same to the goats."

The other two cowpokes broke into laughter. The man speaking sneered and stepped forward one pace to tower over her.

"Let me pass, please."

"Say please with sugar on it. Your backtalk could use a little sweetening."

Ryker set aside his supplies, except for the pick-ax. Then maintaining a suitable distance, he sauntered up the aisle behind Mrs. MacLaren. Not saying a word, he hefted the ax onto his shoulder so the men couldn't miss the wicked implement or the ready and willing to tangle expression he aimed their way.

After a moment's consideration, they stepped aside, and Ryker figured he'd just made three new enemies. The shepherdess seized her opportunity and marched forward to the counter. Quicky paying for her wares, she disappeared out the door. He didn't think she'd seen him standing at her back.

Collecting his supplies, Ryker took his turn to pay. The men closed in. "You're new in town." The largest of the three men did the speaking.

"What's your point."

"You friends with that woman?"

If they only knew. "What if I were?"

"Boss Pritchard don't like her. Which means if you two are friends, he don't like you either."

"And why should I care if Boss Pritchard likes me or not?"

The man straightened to his full height and snagged the toothpick from the side of his mouth. "Because he runs things around here. Her husband learned that the hard way."

Husband… The MacLaren woman having a husband hadn't registered in his mind. It obviously should have. "What happened to him?"

"He's dead. Accidents happen."

Without pressing for further details, Ryker had a feeling regardless of what the doctor had declared on the death certificate, the cause could be attributed to these men.

"Come on, Bearcat. You done said too much." A second man put a hand on Bearcat's shoulder, which Bearcat shrugged off. "If you reckon what's good for you, mister, you'll steer clear of that woman and her property."

The men shuffled past, one purposely bumped into Ryker's shoulder. Another shoved at Ryker's pile of merchandise nearly knocking over the kerosene lantern—the shopkeeper caught the fragile item just in time.

As the ruffians disappeared out the door, Ryker turned toward the man behind the counter. "Nice welcoming party."

"Watch out for that bunch. They're usually up to no good, and capable of just about anything. Irks me no end the way they're always a bothering the Widow MacLaren."

Chapter Three

Una breathed a sigh of relief as her cabin came into view. Her heart always gave a little extra beat at the sight of the sturdy little structure and her happy valley.

Her gaze rose higher to the surrounding foothills and the snowcapped front range looming large in the distance. She marveled at the stalwart folks who crossed those forbidding peaks.

They say another ocean lay on the other side of the divide, as big as the one she journeyed across from Great Britain to America. She was glad Hamish had chosen this place for their home. She had no desire to travel farther west.

Guiding Wallace beneath the overhang beside the cabin, she unhitched and turned him out to pasture. MacTavish barked and whined in happiness, welcoming her home as she stored the newly purchased food stuffs inside her cabin. The creosote and copper sulfate would go in the barn. Although her Angora goats rarely took sick, both products had medicinal purposes and were good to have on hand.

The cattleman-bully in town who called her Miss Sheep Dip wasn't far off. The creosote made a good dip when fleas and lice decided to invade the thick mohair fleeces. But while the rude ruffian might know cattle, the numpty couldn't tell a goat from a sheep.

After covering her beloved cart with a tarp, she set

free the fowl. Their joyful honking and squawking faded as she walked under the cottonwood trees and up onto the ridge to check the beehives.

Fully awake after a long winter's nap, the fuzzy little mites were hungry for pollen. They buzzed about with great purpose traveling to and from the surrounding alfalfa fields and the wild strawberries growing along the creek. She wore no protective covering as the bees never seemed to take notice of her or MacTavish or Wallace.

Last year, a hailstorm destroyed half of one hive, lessening the honey to sell to make ends meet. Make ends meet… She should embroider the refrain on a tattered piece of fabric and hang the quote on the cabin wall. The phrase stood as her watchwords, and the raggedy material represented the usual condition of her wardrobe.

A few steps farther on she stopped to pray beside the solitary boulder marking Hamish's grave. Why or how he had fallen in the canyon remained a mystery. He was surefooted and had traversed the terrain many times. Hamish never believed in the lore surrounding Cougar Rock, yet he'd claimed the craggy ledge as his special place of contemplation. Had dying at the foot of his favorite spot given him a modicum of peace in the hereafter?

Thanks to learning the old ways growing up in Scotland, Una had a knack for perceiving when spirit life inhabited places and objects. Hamish warned she could be shunned for such practices. Like her older brothers, he didn't see eye to eye on her using what Granny Riona had taught her.

Drawing her plaid shawl closer, she rubbed her

cheek against the soft wool. The garment, once her grandmother's, meant the world to Una. The plaid wool, and Celtic necklace hanging inside her cabin, were the only two mementoes from Granny's she'd brought with her to America. Disowned by her brothers, and with her parents and Granny Riona gone to the grave, nothing but memories remained for her in Scotland.

What would Granny have thought of the impending eclipse? Would people in Scotland see the grand cosmic display? All of Colorado, and especially Pike's Peak, was touted to be the best place from which to watch the event. The phenomenon would be seen quite clearly at the farm.

Una wandered over to the Spirit Cave where she'd found the stranger. Worshiped and protected for as far back as time remembered, even the pre-ancestors of the modern-day Indians had held the cave in high esteem.

The native people were mostly gone now, driven out by unreasonable treaties and laws stripping them of their dignity, their rights, and their land. The property she homesteaded once belonged to them, a fact she pondered with no small amount of responsibility. Knowing the history of her valley was another reason she felt a sense of duty to protect the lore and the land with her whole heart and soul.

Mr. Jim, the old vagabond who stopped by on occasion, told her the entire area held mystical energy. And legend stated a powerful treasure was buried in the far reaches of the cave—no doubt the relics the fortune hunter hoped to find.

According to Mr. Jim, the canyon got its name when a young woman, the daughter of a great clan chief, fell in love with a brave promised to another. With a love that wouldn't be denied, the two young people dared to defy their leader and customs.

The shaman of the tribe, uncle to the young brave, helped the couple run away and fulfill what he knew in his heart to be their destiny. They slept their first night as lovers in the Spirit Cave. If one dares to sleep there, you will hear the music of a flute in your dreams—this is your heart song. If you heart is pure the tune will be beautiful, if your heart is troubled so will be the tune. If you hold evil or unkindness in your heart, the music will be frightful, dreadful, abominable.

The next morning, the young couple described to one another the song each had heard, and low and behold the tune had been the same, reaffirming they were meant to be together. Told by the shaman to follow the white panther through the canyon to freedom they waited at the mouth of the cave, and sure enough a mountain lion, white as the snow on the mountain peaks, came to them.

Although they should have been terrified, they did not fear the beast even as the big cat snarled and stared at them with eyes of fire. When he turned and padded silently into the canyon, they jumped up and followed as the shaman had instructed.

When the chief found out what had transpired, he became so angry he killed the holy man as he sat in a trance before his firepit. When the old sage died, the white mountain lion dissolved into mist and smoke leaving the young couple trapped in the canyon, lost to the outside world. A great search was undertaken, costing more lives, but the young lovers were never heard from again. Ashamed of what he'd done, and missing his beloved daughter, and longtime friend, the chief slept one night in the cave. The terrible song he heard drove him to madness, and he died from the terror.

Four hearts had been broken, and Break Heart Canyon earned its name. Since Hamish's death, the legend cut close to home, Una's heart felt broken too. She stared up at Cougar Rock wondering if the mountain lion would ever come to life again.

In Scotland, she'd grown up hearing magical tales of the nine maidens of Dundee, and the Will o' the Wisp. Even her mother swore she once saw the kelpie water horse haunting a lonely river, the gray pony's mane continually dripping water. So why couldn't there be a white panther made of mist and memories?

She'd toyed with the idea of sleeping in the Spirit Cave, but Hamish always refused to join her, and she wasn't brave enough to do so on her own.

****

After storing his purchases in his room, Ryker stopped by to see what was happening at the only saloon in town.

The cowpokes who had hassled him in the general store were present, continuing to act every bit as loud and obnoxious. Because he wanted to keep a low profile, Ryker grabbed a beer at the bar and sought a chair beside a small table at the back of the room.

He wasn't the only one lying low and scoping things out. Another solitary man sat across the way. There was a darkness about him, and not just owing to his black hair, hat, and beard. Pensive and silent, he sat nursing a drink, seemingly oblivious to the rowdy cowboys who gave him a wide berth.

The man they'd called Bearcat at the general store zigzagged his way up to the bar. Obviously drunk, he could barely order another beer and a shot of whiskey. When the barkeep hesitated, the belligerent man slammed his hand down on the counter demanding service.

"Come on, Bearcat," one of his buddies cajoled. "We got a long night ahead of us. We need you to be awake for the doin's."

"Oh yeah, I forgot. That little lady will sure be surprised come morning."

At this bit of information, Ryker perked up. Were they talking about Mrs. MacLaren? He'd already planned on visiting her property tonight. If these no accounts showed up, he might come across more than a lost treasure.

****

Ryker had been exploring the cave for hours. Using the limited light of the lantern, the going was slow.

Deciding to take a break, he exited the cave and sat at the entrance, his back against the rocks as he enjoyed a few deep breaths of cool evening air. Besides providing insufficient light the kerosene lamp seemed to suck all the air from the cavern, and the fumes made his eyes burn.

None of the information supplied gave the slightest hint as to how to proceed once he'd located the cavern—he was playing it by ear. Eating the apple he brought along, he visualized what he'd found so far. The first chamber was of medium size yet roomy enough to allow him to stand erect and walk around. The second chamber he'd painstakingly discovered was more impressive. Squeezing through a fissure barely allowing for his size, Ryker couldn't believe what was revealed on the other side. A larger hollowed out area with a cathedral-like ceiling met his gaze. Here, the darkness was complete.

The pictograph on the far wall reminded him of the rock pictures he'd seen in the caves of Africa. Those renderings were considered works of art and told a story. These marks were structured, like words or symbols. A warning perhaps?

Tossing aside the apple core for a forest creature, Ryker gained his feet and stretched and fought off the urge to fall asleep. As he walked the well-worn path running from the cave to the fence line, he reckoned by the position of the moon, the midnight hour had come and gone.

The whinny of a horse brought him up short. Thankfully, his horse, tethered across the river, didn't answer. Stepping behind the shelter of a group of aspens, Ryker waited. About twenty yards away, faint moonlight highlighted three figures on horseback. In the still of the night, as they dismounted on the far side of Mrs. MacLaren's fence, their talk and laughter filtered over to him.

Most of the goats were settled down in the lower pasture between the river and her cabin. Their bright white hair making them easy to spot.

The men cut the fence wires and began rocking the wooden posts back and forth to loosen them. If he had to make a guess, he'd say the biggest man, grunting and working at the destruction of property, was Bearcat. Another of the strangers re-mounted, and guiding his horse through the new opening, he headed directly for the goats and herded them back through the cut fence.

By morning the animals will have strayed deep into the surrounding forest.

Where was that blasted dog of hers? Why wasn't he setting up a ruckus and taking on these no accounts? Probably for the best, at any interference these brutes would most likely shoot the creature. With the goats set free and run off, the other two men mounted up and all three disappeared into the night.

Ryker retraced his steps to the cave entrance, and dug through his survival pack until he unearthed a bundle of rope. Moving quietly so as not to spook the goats farther into the trees, he circled around the cluster of animals and herded them back through the fence to their pasture. Most of them went readily enough and he figured the ones he missed would stay close to the main group until morning.

Propping up the listing post, he ran three lengths of rope horizontally across the opening where the fence was missing. Then he crisscrossed several loops between the ropes. With any luck, the temporary repair should last until the woman noticed the problem.

Remaining cloaked in the desire to take a nap as he retraced his steps to the cave, an image of Una MacLaren popped into his weary mind. Was she sleeping peacefully half an acre away while this mischief had taken place? Was he any better than Bearcat and his partners? He was taking advantage of her slumber as well, committing his own brand of mischief.

****

Sitting in the dark at the kitchen table, Una sipped the cold tea leftover in the pot. A message had come to her in her sleep. Not the first time she'd had guidance from beyond, so she knew better than to ignore the warning.

She'd gotten up and checked around outside. The herd had wandered to the far fence line, but they didn't seem in distress. Exploring a bit farther, she'd felt nothing amiss, and mystified, she'd returned.

MacTavish was locked in the barn guarding the nanny who had delivered late in the season and the sickly kid showing signs of distress. Tomorrow night, she would sleep in the barn and leave MacTavish free to wander.

Setting aside her tea, she idly plucked at the curly ends of her braid. A few more hours of sleep was still possible, and she could use them. But although her body ached for the feather bed, her mind whirred like the wheels of a clockwork toy.

She thought about the man she'd surprised in the cave. How dare he trespass, and worse yet suggest she take money to allow him to desecrate the relics buried here. He was braw for a haughty vagabond, though. Duine brèagha, a handsome man indeed.

She smiled. Then finding the territory unfamiliar due to lack of use, the smile slipped away.

Chapter Four

"What happened here little lady?"

Una spun around and dropped the hammer she held as she grabbed her rifle. Her leather boots cushioned the blow when the heavy tool hit the toe of her right foot.

"Simmer down, it's only me." Mr. Jim took a step back.

"By the Saints, you scared me halfway to the grave." Una lowered the hammer on the rifle and set the weapon aside. Then she scolded MacTavish. "Just because we know Mr. Jim is no reason not to alert me when he's approaching.

"And to be answering your question, some ne'er-do-well cut my fence. Then by the looks of things, somebody else bound the wires back together. A good thing too, or my goats would be long gone into the free land, and who knows what lives out there. I have them all back, the stray ones remained close by."

"That's mighty curious doin's. Let me give you a hand to make things right. Sorry I gave you a fright. I'll whistle a tune next time I'm passing by so you can hear me coming."

"I would appreciate your consideration." Una enjoyed the occasional company of Whiskey Jim, or Mr. Jim as she preferred to call him. But she didn't like surprises.

Among other job descriptions, he declared himself

a prospector and local tour guide. Based upon their limited conversations, she'd say he had many an adventure to tell wrapped in a good bit of education, which he tried not to flaunt. He certainly knew the history and legends of the area, especially Break Heart Canyon. How he'd come to be called Whiskey Jim had yet to be revealed.

Regardless of why he showed up today, she thanked providence. Repairing a fence was a two-person job, and together they were made short work of the difficult task.

"I reckon who caused the trouble isn't a great mystery." Jim didn't glance up from the wire he twisted around a nail. "But who fixed it, now there's a question to ponder."

"Tis a mystery to be sure. Maybe taking pity on a poor Scottish lass down on her luck, the wee folk sent the fae to lend a hand."

"Now there's a fanciful idea. But you're rich in many ways, child, at least in the ones that count."

Una routinely gave thanks for the good things in her life, especially at night for a day gone well. But *rich* rarely entered her mind, even as a future possibility.

"I know such platitudes don't help if you go to bed hungry or without a new dress, but it's true."

Refusing to feel the slightest bit sorry for herself, a condition she fought against with vigor, she changed the subject. "So, what news do you bring from your travels of late."

"The coming solar event is on most people's minds." Mr. Jim straightened from his labors to momentarily stare up at the sky. "They say you should wear darkening glasses to view the spectacle lest you'll

32

go blind."

"Goodness me. What about the animals."

"Apparently, they're smart enough not to look. Which says more for their intelligence than ours."

"I have a piece of smoked glass, will that do?"

"I wouldn't chance it. I'll try to find us the proper eyewear of amber glass. Or we can rig up a big tub of clear calm water and watch the reflection as if it were a mirror. Kathleen, over at the school, is assembling pin hole boxes for the children, because sure enough one of them is going to try staring right at the spectacle, and you can hardly blame them."

"After all this hoopla, we better be prayin' for clear weather."

"Prayers couldn't hurt. We'll be the laughingstock of the nation if it's cloudy on the big day. The United States Congress appropriated $8,000 for eclipse observations. Can you imagine that? They're usually taking our money not handing it out. And the Pennsylvania Railroad Company is giving professional astronomers half-price fare from the East Coast to Denver."

"This event has stirred the passions of people around the world. Even our little city is embracing the excitement. The invading hordes should be doin' wonders for your tourist guiding business."

Mr. Jim laughed at her comment. "I'll be busy as popcorn on a skillet." He took a big kerchief from his pocket and wiped his brow. "I hear Thomas Edison opted for Wyoming. I would have liked to meet him. And several expeditions are heading for Texas. But the majority of scientists and astronomers are setting up in Colorado. There's even an observatory on the roof of the Teller House in Central City, and one posh hotel in Colorado Springs has hired a band to entertain guests as they watch the solar display"

As Mr. Jim rambled on, Una removed her straw hat and fanned her face. The sun had climbed high, and the work had been hard. She needed a breather as she listened to the information Mr. Jim imparted. The alignments of the stars and the moon were important to her. Even now, far from her homeland, Una celebrated the solstices and the equinoxes and special Celtic holidays.

"How are things on Pikes Peak?" she asked, when Mr. Jim stopped talking. "I hear one gentleman is not faring well."

"Yes, Cleveland Abbe. He's a meteorologist. Altitude sickness has hit him hard. He's part of Samuel Pierpont Langley's team. They made their camp at the very summit. He came down for a while. Then he insisted they carry him back up on a stretcher."

"There is definitely a wee bit of madness taking over. People either have their heads in the clouds or they're digging for bones in the dirt. Like the fellow I caught looking for artifacts in the cave—

"When was this?" Seeming upset, Mr. Jim uncharacteristically interrupted her midsentence.

"Two days ago. MacTavish and I ran him off. But I've a feeling he's the persistent kind."

"What exactly was he looking for?"

"Those din-o-saur bones. Said he'd heard a rumor about the canyon, and he'd pay handsome for information and permission to search the cave."

"What did he look like?" Mr. Jim's eyes narrowed, and he stood tall with his hands clenched into fists as if ready for a fight. Usually easy going, Una had never before seen this side of his personality.

"The man was slightly taller than you, with brown hair burnished in the sun, and brown eyes able to catch one's attention." Now why had she described him in such a way? He was a drifter, and whether or not his eyes held humor and the promise of adventure, he shouldnae mean anything to her, and wasn't worth wasting time over descriptive phrases. Yet his image was embedded in her mind. "Oh, and he wore a leather hat which had seen better days but was set at a cocky angle matching his cocky attitude."

"Hmm. Your description leads me to believe there are two of them."

"Two of what?"

"Mercenaries from the Bone Wars brigades. They're ruthless, would do anything for the money they're being paid. Don't mind so much if they nose around up by Garden Park, the bones truly are a curiosity, but we don't need them digging up the past and trespassing on private property."

"Describe the other man to which you refer."

"Tall, with black hair and a disposition to match. Seen him around town a few times. He was also asking questions about Break Heart Canyon, so keep an eye out for him as well."

This sounded like the same man her friend had described, the one Kate's husband, Jordie, had assisted at the bank.

"MacTavish and I promise to be vigilant. At least the townspeople are making a few dollars off the flood of curio seekers. They're selling objects they've collected over the years, lots of arrow heads and trade goods, many items found while plowing up the fields. I only have one precious keepsake. A geode. On the day we were wed, my husband surprised me with that rock filled with the most beautiful purple crystals. I'll nae be selling such a memento without good cause."

"A thoughtful gift. I regret not being around more while Hamish was still alive. You've done admirably since his passing. When I lost my wife, I lost my mind and my way, wasting precious time searching for the meaning of life."

This was the first time Mr. Jim had mentioned being married and a widower, which explained the haunted sadness in his eyes. She wished to hear more, but knew firsthand not to pry into such sorrow. "Your suffering must go deep. Hamish found the stone in the Spirit Cave the one time he ventured inside."

"Makes the gift even more special. Have you slept in there yet?"

"Nae. I'm not brave enough. Although I'd like to try."

"You'll know when the time is right."

"The heart song legend you told me reminds me of the myths of Scotland, only we would have thrown in a donnie or a grogan."

"What pray tell are those?"

"The Fae. You call them faeries and brownies."

"Well don't worry, there's plenty of magical doin's about without faeries. But tales of enchantment can also turn tragic."

"Aye, 'tis the same in Scotland. How do you know so much about all the memories locked away in this canyon?"

"My family lived here for generations. My

grandfather stayed with the Utes. Even fought alongside them against other tribes. Those were times of glory and freedom. Then the soldiers came to take them away to the reservations. Those were sad times—and still are. There won't be any coming back to what this frontier once was. But these myths and tales began long before the existence of the tribes we now recognize."

Again, Una realized Mr. Jim wasn't your run of the mill prospector, trail guide. "I think you are pretending to be a down and out drifter, but your true calling is the stewardship of the land and legends."

Mr. Jim appeared taken aback at having the pretense of his lifestyle exposed, but he quickly recovered. "The task seems an inherited trait." There was passion in his voice.

With a plaintive bleat, a kid goat sprinted closer chewing and sucking on the edge of Una's plaid shawl. Before long, three more white fluffy babes with pink noses and hangy-down ears joined the first. Una shooed them away.

"I love you to pieces, bonny wee bairns, but you must go find your mother for your lunchtime feeding. You'll not get much nourishment from my twisted fringe." As they scampered off full of playful antics, she and Mr. Jim had a hardy laugh.

"How's the wool business going by the way?"

"Now days, to sell locally is my only hope. Shipping the raw mohair or the clothing I make has become frightfully expensive. I have few takers for warm clothes in the summer heat, but business will pick up when winter threatens. Everything has its season."

"Indeed. Even love."

****

"We did what you said, boss. But when we checked back from afar just before dawn, somebody had rounded up the animals and temporarily fixed the fence."

"Find out who the interloper was and take care of them. And if you don't see signs or hear-tell that obstinate female and her goats are moving on, you better follow through with the next plan on your agenda.

"Okay, boss."

"Well then, get to it."

Curly Joe gladly exited Mr. Pritchard's office and met up with Bearcat who was waiting on the porch. "Was he mad?"

"He wasn't happy. We're to check things out, and if she ain't leaving in a couple of days, we need to come up with a new means of driving her out."

"Hard to believe the poison didn't work. I didn't like doing that, not even to those smelly sheep."

"You know they're goats not sheep, and what matters is how much you'd like keepin' your job. We're also supposed to find out who fixed the fence."

"With all the doin's going on around here, there's a stranger behind every bush, including a few rough customers. Ones who look like they shoot back."

"Stop your whining, Bearcat. You're getting soft in your old age."

"That's the point. I'd like to enjoy my old age and not git kilt because of another of Mr. Pritchard's hairbrained schemes. We already did more for him than I care to remember or admit to."

"He won't stop until he owns all the land betwixt his property and the creek coming out of Break Heart

Canyon. And that woman is what's standing in his way."

"I don't like going anywhere near the gorge. There're things up there ain't natural."

"What are you goin' on about?"

"Silas and I went cougar hunting up there once. We spent the night to get an early start in the morning. A couple of hours after sundown, the spooky noises commenced."

"What kind of noises?"

"First came the voices. We searched around camp but couldn't find sign of anybody. And every time we went lookin' in one direction, the sounds come from another. We couldn't understand the words they was a sayin, Silas declared it was Indian talk. Then we heard a cougar screamin`. A big, mean, none too happy at having his territory invaded cougar.

"The way the sound echoed down the canyon, we had to cover our ears or lose our minds. When the ordeal stopped, we packed up in the dark and lit out. And while we were stumbling out of there, over rock and fallen limbs, we saw flashes of white between the trees and the sound of an animal breathing heavy. The noise followed us all the way down to Strawberry Creek and across the backside of the MacLaren property."

Curly Joe turned around expecting to see a comical expression on Bearcat's face reassuring him the story he'd just heard was nothing but a tall tale. Instead, Curly Joe saw frightened eyes claiming the story was true.

"Maybe we won't have to go back there in the dark. She can't last much longer being on her own and all."

Chapter Five

Ryker jerked awake and leapt to his feet.

His pulse slowed as he remembered where he was. The cave—his second night in the cave. He only meant to sit down for a moment and must have drifted off.

This working at night was killing him. He was a morning bird, not a night owl. And he'd had a nightmare—one he hoped never to have again. His heart ramped back up at the memory.

The beginning of the dream had been comforting with swirling colors and the gentle melody of a flutelike instrument. Then the fear and darkness had come, with voices shouting in anger as the tune turned deafening and wild. The dream had felt so real, and the remnants of the sound and fury still seemed to hover in the cave sending him outside and into the night air.

According to the pocket watch he'd remembered to bring along, the time was nearly four a.m. Dang, he'd slept for two hours. The morning light would soon be here, he'd better get back to work.

Shaking off the feeling of unease, he reentered the cave, and holding the kerosene lantern in front of him, he squeezed through the opening and into the second cavern. Running his hand over the cool dampness of cracks and fissures, he came upon an out of place, irregular rock he hadn't before noticed. Retrieving the knife from the scabbard at his waist, he chipped away at the sides until he could get a grip on the stone. Tugging and pulling with all his might, he stumbled backward when it came loose.

Casting aside the rock, he wedged his hand and arm through the newly formed opening. There was empty space beyond—empty space and what else? Fear of the unknown washed over him, and he jerked his arm free and retreated, dusting his hands together as if shedding off any bad luck clinging to them.

With hopes of widening the small opening, he returned to the main cavern for the pick-ax. As he reached for the tool, a menacing growl stopped him. Investigating the sound, Ryker came face to face with MacTavish, teeth barred and blocking the entrance of the cave.

Anticipating a run-in with Mrs. MacLaren's guard dog, at breakfast yesterday morning, Ryker had saved part of the steak accompanying his eggs. Moving ever so slowly, he slid his hand into the pocket of his vest and retrieved a sliver of meat from the oil cloth in which he'd wrapped the treat.

"Hey there, MacTavish, you're out early this morning. Here, are you hungry?" He tossed the scrap to the dog who sniffed suspiciously at the delicacy. Ryker generally had a way with animals, but this one seemed specifically loyal to his owner and the land. "I mean you no harm, boy. And I agree, your mistress is indeed worthy of protection. But a man's got to make a living, you understand."

MacTavish wolfed down the meat but didn't relinquish his position or attitude. Ryker tossed out another chunk. The second piece disappeared, the unwavering stare from haunting golden eyes remained.

The standoff continued as soft morning light edged into the cave. The bray of a donkey filled the air, and when MacTavish heard his mistress call, the dog took off never looking back.

Extinguishing the kerosene lamp, Ryker grabbed what equipment he could, and splashing across Strawberry Creek, he made a beeline toward his horse. After securing what he carried, he mounted up and headed into the cover of the woods.

What bad luck. He was sure he'd located the secret chamber housing the item for which he searched. Waiting until tonight for further exploration would be excruciatingly hard, but he could use the time to get over the effects of the dream/nightmare. The incident had rattled him to the core, and like a slow burn, the uneasy feeling continued to harry the edges of his mind. Something untoward was going on here.

The world held many beliefs not easily explained. He'd witnessed voodoo rituals in Haiti, illusions performed by mystics in India, and the magic of a shaman in China. Mystical forces weaving their way through Mrs. MacLaren's property wasn't totally out of the realm of possibilities. Too bad she couldn't use them against the cattlemen who seemed bound and determined to cause her trouble. Or maybe he could use them to persuade her to relinquish the treasure.

A sound echoed in the woods. His mount remained calm, so Ryker ruled out a predatory animal—but not a predatory human. Risking being silhouetted against the sky, he directed the gelding up onto a rise studded with trees. Stopping beside a large fir, he turned to observe the valley below.

Loping across an open area, riding north toward

town, a mounted figure dressed in black came into view…the man from Caňon City. According to rumor, he was a bone hunter by the name of Dax Thompson. Did he know about the ancient breast plate Mr. Cockrell hired Ryker to find?

If the relic truly existed, more than one rich elitist would be drooling to get his hands on the prize. The need to own such objects made men do and pay for strange things, and Ryker happily took their money to fulfill their obsessions. Except when it came to war— war was the obsession of men gone mad. Then he always chose to fight on the side of the underdog, regardless of how much money the other side offered.

The man disappeared out of sight, seemingly intent on keeping going. Ryker glanced toward the shadowed cleft hiding the cave entrance. As annoying as MacTavish could be, he hoped the stalwart beast would keep watch in case the man in black returned.

****

"What's the matter, laddie? Where were you when I called?"

Una petted MacTavish and stroked his ears. Since the fence incident, she jumped at every untoward noise, fearing a boogeyman hid behind each tree and bush. But the goats grazed happily in the morning sun and the meadow larks tweeted uninterrupted.

With a shake of her head to chase away the peelie-wallies, she ambled over to the barn and made sure Wallace had clean water in his trough. Then as Bitsy the barn cat observed from the loft, she checked on the nanny and sickly kid cozied in the near stall.

The sweet babe had floppy kid syndrome. Una mixed up another cup of water and baking soda. Then twisting the corner of a clean cloth into a teat, she dipped the fabric into the solution and allowed the kid to suckle on the material. The treatment appeared to be working, and the kid showed more strength, struggling upright with a wee bit more success. Sitting on a bale of hay beside the wabbling darling, she supported the little body against her leg and continued the feeding.

To lose even one animal made a significant dent in her mohair business, and no matter how good she took care of her goats, older animals eventually passed away, or one would get snake bit, or wander too far from MacTavish's protection to be taken by a coyote. Consequently, every new addition to her herd was important—offsetting the inevitable. And old or newborn, losing them hurt her heart immeasurably. After Hamish died, she declared she had no heart left which with to love again—apparently there was enough left to hurt anew.

At the sound of whistling, she gained her feet, set aside the baking soda mix, and stepped out into the open. MacTavish came tearing around the corner, woofing softly, before standing alert at her side.

Movement in the nearby cottonwood trees caught her attention, and Mr. Jim emerged from the shadows. True to his word he'd whistled so as not to sneak up on her unawares.

She raised a hand in recognition. The melody ceased and breathing heavily he drew close. "Thank goodness you saw me. I'm too old to clamber around these parts while carrying on a tune."

"Aye, I see it's taking a great toll on you, but the effort is appreciated. Set yourself down. I've clean water here." She offered up what she'd brought along to make the baking soda slurry. Mr. Jim didn't hesitate to reach for the water and down a good portion.

"I didna expect to be seeing you again so soon."

"You mentioned wanting another donkey to keep Wallace company, and I heard of a little gray jenny which sounded like she'd fill the bill."

"How wonderful, Mr. Jim. Thank you. Wallace needs a friend." Hearing his name, the donkey huffed and whined and reached his head over the rail, eyes wide and ears on the alert. "You'd like some company wouldn't you, boy?" Una scratched him under his chin sending his lower lip sagging in ecstasy.

"Everybody needs a somebody." Mr. Jim nodded in agreement.

"What was your Mrs. Jim like?" Una was not only curious, she understood talking about those we've lost helped to keep the memories alive.

The light of interest flickered in Jim's eyes, and he seemed eager to share today. "She was a grand lady who put up with me for more years than I care to admit to. No shrinking violet, she could give as well as she got, mind you. She was proud of her extensive vocabulary, and we loved to parry words. She could talk the bark off a tree."

He chuckled and blinked several times as if chasing away the threat of tears. "Sometimes I'd support the offside in a discussion just to get her started explaining why she was correct. But she always caught on quick enough, then we'd laugh. I miss laughing, it's the balm to the pains of life."

"I ken what you're saying. When I come upon something which tickles me, I tell MacTavish or Wallace, and they politely listen, but act like they think

I'm daft. Special recollections are hard too. When a happy memory occurs, there's no one on Earth to whom you can say *remember when*."

"Well, if I managed to find a friend for this funny fellow, surely someone is out there waiting for you." He gave Wallace a pat on the neck.

"You've more faith than I in the in the whims of Fate. Tell me more about this bonnie lady donkey. Why is she for sale and how much will she be costing me."

"This is word of mouth mind you, but I'm told she's a right good size so can help with the work and has even been ridden a bit."

"She'd have a good home here. How much?"

"Ten dollars."

Her high hopes took a dive. "Aye there's the rub then. To come up with the fee, I'll be needing to part with something of value." In her mind's eye she inventoried the house for an item worth such a price. The geode Hamish had given her was the obvious choice. A shop in town had offered her twice that amount when they evaluated her treasure. But could she part with the keepsake? To decide this quickly made her stomach clench. "I have to think on it."

"I'll tell the owner you're interested. I know you'll find a way. She's only four years old so there's lots of life left in her. She needs you as much as you need her."

Mr. Jim made saying no near to impossible, and the opportunity sounded golden. Most donkeys she saw around the area were sad specimens, old and worn from years of prospecting. Another such offer may not come again soon. She had to make this work. "Oh, all right, I'll take her. But the seller must give me a few days. Where would I have to go to meet him?"

"If you'll let me, I can take care of the transaction. He's located out in a tangle of woods to the south. I'm not sure it's the best place for a lady to be travelling alone."

The area to which he referred was a wild place full of scallywags and ruffians with rumors illegal distillation of hard spirits took place there on a regular basis. Knowing where the donkey came from made her wish she could rescue her even more quickly. But Granny Riona warned about buying a pig in a poke. She wouldn't see the animal until the money was gone. Was blindly trusting in Mr. Jim a good idea?

Trust—a shopworn commodity. She trusted her husband would live a long life. She trusted she would be allowed to live here in peace. She'd trusted in the Celtic gods and goddesses from her childhood, and the Christian God she'd learned about as an adult. Yet every time, her trust and faith seemed misplaced or ignored. Still, she really wanted another donkey.

Mr. Jim had helped her last winter when her sledge sunk so deep into the snow even Wallace couldn't pull the sleigh free. And the man stopped one day and split wood for her—at his age perhaps not an activity he should be doing. She studied his kind face. In her heart she felt he would do her no harm.

"I want the donkey." There, she'd gone and said it and there was no turning back.

"Good. I don't think you'll be disappointed. Oh, and would you mind if I set up camp for the night at the mouth of the cave? I find comfort there by the canyon."

"Of course, you may. You're always welcome on my property. I must say you're one of the few who finds ease of mind near the twisted maze of cliffs and superstitions."

Una was aware Mr. Jim often slept at the mansion size house peering down from the nearby hills. In exchange, he ran errands and kept the place up for the owner, whom no one had seen in years. Mr. Jim's request to stay on her patch of land rather than the fancy doings yonder made her happy.

Chapter Six

What was he going to do all day?

When Ryker clandestinely returned to the cave last night, he found an old man camped out front. His plans waylaid, he'd returned to Cañon City where he'd played a few hands of poker at the saloon. Then he went to bed.

Now his sleep-by-day work-by-night routine had gone topsy-turvy, and his visions of unearthing a great discovery behind the hole in the wall were upended again. He wondered how long the man intended to stay there?

The elderly interloper appeared to be the scraggly ne'er do well Ryker had seen around town. Discovering him living rough by the cave demanded further investigation. Were Mrs. MacLaren and the mighty MacTavish aware of this trespasser? For such a peaceful little valley, there sure were a lot of comings and goings on that woman's property.

As Ryker strolled along the boardwalk this morning, his shoulders twitched with the desire to wield the pickax and smash through the cave wall. Of course, he knew working carefully and methodically was the way to go, but the longer he considered the possibilities of what could be waiting inside, the greater the excitement built in his body. Like holding a winning poker hand with one more ante to go, the thrill ran high.

Hopefully, the old man would be gone tonight.

As the sun blazed unfettered, Ryker decided to take a moment of respite in the cool shelter of the Cañon City Western Union office. Might as well send his employer a telegram.

A rotund lady with a straw-hat drenched in paper flowers stood at the counter. "One dollar, please ma'am." The clerk requested payment, and the woman counted out the appropriate coinage. After a brisk thank you and a good day, she left, and Ryker stepped up to take her place.

"What can I do for you, mister?" Wrought iron bars framed the wiry man behind the raised counter. Standing at attention, his right hand tapped the counter as if he simultaneously coded the words he spoke.

"Howdy. I'd like to send this information to New York City to be delivered to the address indicated." Written previously on a precious scrap of paper torn from his journal, Ryker slid the parchment across the wood panel and into the hands of the clerk

Ryker's boss, Mr. Cockrell, had requested routine updates on his progress, and for once Ryker had good news, or almost good news. He was sure the hidden area contained something of value, and by hinting at the discovery, he hoped his boss might send a few dollars his way. If nothing was revealed, he wouldn't have actually lied to get the stipend.

"Are you sure you got the name spelled correctly?" Peering with interest through his wire-rimmed glasses, the man studied the missive.

"What do you mean?

"The fellow who came in yesterday also sent a message to the same name at the same place. He only put one L in Cockrel."

"Another fellow? A big guy riding a roan gelding? Black hair, black hat?"

"I don't recall what horse he was riding, but the rest tallies."

"Far as I know, it's two L's in Cockrell. What did his message say?"

"Can't tell you. Just like I wouldn't tell him what you wrote should he ask."

The determined set of the clerk's jaw discouraged Ryker from asking a second time.

"I can appreciate your ethics."

This was a curious happenstance. What was Cockrell up to? Had he hired two men to find the same artifact? The prospect made little sense, but did explain why the other man had been sniffing around Break Heart Canyon and the cave. Not a coincidence after all.

"Make it two Ls."

"The customer is always right." After transferring the information to an official form, the clerk returned the scrap of paper and asked Ryker to verify everything had been copied correctly.

"Looks good. Can money be wired to the bank here in Cañon City?"

"Yes, sir. Western Union's been wire-transferring greenbacks and coinage since 1872. That'll be a dollar and twenty-five cents."

"But you only charged the lady a dollar."

"She only sent a message to Chicago. Cost more to go all the way to New York." He gave a shrug and held up his hands as if he had no control over the pricing. "Company's still paying off the transcontinental line they put in."

Business was business, no use arguing. Ryker handed over the fee. He'd been thrifty and had enough money to live on with a little left over. And if Cockrell didn't send any advance, he could go back to living out of doors. Then his expenses would be even less.

"I'll check back with you on occasion for a reply."

"That'll work." The clerk nodded goodbye.

Returning to the boardwalk Ryker took a moment to glance around. There were parts of the town he'd yet to explore, might as well fill the day nosing around and getting the lay of the land. He went to step out into the street then hesitated and drew back when a figure across the way caught his attention. Mrs. MacLaren was standing in front of the local curio shop, her brazen pink cart hitched nearby. She held an object close to her chest and kept glancing at the object and then at the door to the store. Twice she made to walk into the establishment, but each time she faltered and turned back. Finally, after glancing heavenward, she squared her shoulders and marched in without hesitation.

A short time later, she came out clutching her purse but not the item she'd carried in. Glancing neither left or right she went straight to her cart, climbed aboard, and went down the street in a slow and somber manner. Shoulders slumped, she appeared downhearted.

Ryker crossed the street and entered the curio shop.

As he weaved his way down the nearest aisle of bric-a-brac, the proprietor hovered at his back as if he feared Ryker might pick up an item, and not put it back down.

"Looking for anything particular?" the owner asked as they returned to the front of the store.

"Not really. Have you anything new and

interesting?"

"This came in just moments ago." The man indicated a large purple geode sitting on the counter.

Mesmerized by the dazzling crystals, Ryker couldn't resist reaching for the rock. The owner's hand shot out preventing any such familiarity with his newest prize.

Trying not to appear interested, Ryker stuck his hands in his pockets, and again leisurely strolled around the store. Circling back once again, he placed his hands on the counter, one on each side of the geode.

"How much?"

"Well, I've hardly had time to consider a price."

"I'm in no hurry."

"Thirty dollars."

"Twenty."

"But that's what I gave the lady who brought in the geode. I'd be making no profit at all."

"I bet you make a pretty good profit on the masks hanging in the corner. You claim they're rare and from the mysterious continent of Darkest Africa. I say they're *hecho en Mexico,* amigo. I've lived in both places.

"Twenty dollars will be fine."

"And a box, please."

With a grumble of resignation, the owner complied.

Package in hand, Ryker stood just outside the door. A quick scan of the street told him the pink cart and Mrs. MacLaren were long gone. Hefting the box, he wondered why he'd bought the pricey object. If Cockrell didn't come through with a bit of money, he'd be eating beans for a week, and passing wind for two.

****

Head down, ears drooping, Wallace plodded along as if he picked up on Una's sadness.

"We can't keep to the past," she said, more to bolster herself than the donkey. "It's the only way we can survive the future. And if nobody purchases our geode, I can buy the prize back this fall when my woolen items sell.

"Besides, you should be happy. We'll give half the money to Mr. Jim this afternoon, and soon he will bring you a wonderful lady donkey to be your friend."

Guiding Wallace off the main road, they took the two-track leading to her property. She should give the farm a name. Everything else around here had a title of sorts. Break Heart Canyon, the Spirit Cave, Strawberry Creek, Cougar Rock. But nothing came to mind. She dearly loved the land but had yet to spiritually connect to her surroundings.

She'd done a sage smudge on the cabin and found comfort there at night. But unrest lurked in the shadows outside, especially in the canyon as if the towering rocks could find no peace. There were spirits waiting to be revealed and set to right. Until then, even the sunlight couldn't drive away the darkness in the canyon.

"Whoa now, Wallace." Reaching the barn they stopped, and MacTavish bounded over. The herd appeared happy and grazing, and MacTavish's carefree attitude reassured her nothing untoward had occurred in her absence.

Unhitching the cart, she settled Wallace in the pasture. "You're a good and stalwart laddie." After his long walk, she rewarded him with high praise and a tidbit of sweet feed.

With the dog at her heels, she entered the cabin, removed her hat, and checked on the bread dough she'd left rising in the sunny window. The wild strawberries by the creek were ripe, and there were a few blueberries left on the bushes as well. She should bake pies this week too.

Punching down the dough, she divided the mound in half, kneaded both pieces several times then placed each in a bread pan. Covered with a clean tea towel, back in the sun they went.

She loaded the wood stove in preparation for baking but held off on starting a fire. The bread would take at least another hour for the second rise, maybe more. In the meantime, there was plenty of mending to do.

She stitched a hole in the sleeve of Hamish's flannel shirt—her favorite, the one she wore at night after the chores were done for the day and she removed her *fragrant* barn clothes. She loved curling up in his remembered warmth.

As she finished the last stitch, the sound of whistling could be heard.

Jumping up she met Mr. Jim outside, and hesitating only a moment, she handed over the agreed upon precious ten dollars.

"It's a sound transaction," he reassured Una. "And I promise to return as soon as possible with the newest addition to your menagerie. I might need to linger a while, rushing off can be interpreted as unfriendly. These are not folks you want to insult or have as enemies."

"Mr. Jim, I didn't realize you were putting yourself

in danger to procure my donkey. Maybe it's not such a good idea."

"Nonsense. As in most things, just have to proceed with respect and caution."

Proceeding with caution seemed her watch word, which Kate declared made life exceedingly dull.

Chapter Seven

Ryker watched the old man head off into the woods to the south. Today he moved with purpose rather than ambling along without direction.

Taking advantage of the fellow's absence, Ryker stepped around the man's campsite, and with rucksack and hammer in hand, he slipped into the cave and darkness.

The kerosene lamp still waited for his match. Entering the second chamber, and holding high the light, Ryker sought the opening in the wall. There wasn't one. Searching frantically, he discovered the area had been patched. Had he not been familiar with the area, he would never have known where to look.

Was this the effort of the old man? A bit of a chill licked at the nape of his neck, and again the sensation of being watched had him glancing over his shoulder. Shaking off the feeling, he tapped and hammered at the wall. With little effort, the fragile new patch crumbled away in a cloud of dust revealing the original opening. Brushing the fragments from his face and hands, he returned to the main chamber for his canteen. Then he froze at the sound of scuffling right outside.

Keeping to the shadows of the main chamber, Ryker slipped the Colt revolver free from his holster. A man stood at the cave entrance. Light streamed in from behind the intruder hindering Ryker's view of his face, but from what he could make out, the figure was Dax Thompson.

Ryker stepped forward. "This cave's off limits."

The man crouched ready for action, one hand on the butt of his revolver. Then apparently noticing Ryker had the drop on him, he lowered his hand, not making a play for the gun. "Says who?" He spat out the words like he wished they were bullets.

"Says me."

"And who the hell are you to tell me what to do."

"I'm just another of Cockrell's boys, doing his bidding." Ryker hoped if the stranger knew they were working for the same brand, he might ease off.

"Nothing like a little competition to add to the excitement."

"Or you could mosey along and find another cave to stick your nose into."

"Got to follow orders, just like you."

So Cockrell really had hired two men to find the same artifact, doubling his chances of success with no concern for what trouble he might stir up. Aware of his boss' propensity for making wagers, he guessed the man had placed bets with his snobbish friends as to which of them would find the prize first.

"Then it sounds like we've got a problem."

"Correction, you've got a problem."

Deciding to take a chance, the man leaped to one side as he went for his gun. A bullet whizzed past Ryker's head striking the wall and chipping off a shard of rock. The splinter pierced his shoulder like a knife blade. Teeth clenched in pain, Ryker fired back and ran to the mouth of the cave.

The man had disappeared from view. Then he

caught a flash of movement in the boulders off to his left. Another shot rang out—another near miss. Ryker tore through the old man's campsite, kicking the frying pan and bedroll out of the way. Wedging himself behind two sturdy aspen trees, he waited for the man in black to make the next move.

The stranger had chosen poorly as far as direction. Unless privy to the secret path rumored to exist, there was nothing behind the man but a blind canyon. And nothing in front of him but Ryker—who was sorely pissed off and ready to defend his find.

Beneath his shirt, blood trickled down from the shoulder wound. He slowed his breathing and tried to ignore the pain. The sound of rocks being disturbed echoed in the chasm, and Ryker pictured his enemy scrambling around, exploring the possibility of a nearby exit. Then another sound sent a chill down his spine.

"MacTavish, come back, you dastardly hound."

Mrs. MacLaren and the dog must have heard the shots. Between the tree branches, he saw flashes of long red hair. She was heading straight for danger. He called out, but the barking of the dog masked his warning. Seeing no alternative, he left the safety of the twin aspens and ran across the open space to the cottonwood trees she traversed. With every step, he tensed with the expectation of a bullet striking him in the back.

"It's all right, buddy. It's just me." Ryker frantically searched his pocket but found no treats for the oncoming dog. MacTavish leaped and growled in a highly unfriendly manner. When Mrs. MacLaren reached his side, she grabbed hold of the hound and calmed him down.

"You must turn back," Ryker ordered. "There's a

stranger near the mouth of the canyon. And he's dangerous."

"You're a stranger too," she countered.

Oddly, after spending so many hours in the area, he'd begun to feel he belonged here.

"He doesn't care if you get hurt—I do."

Her lips parted in surprise, then settled into a grim line of realization.

All debate ended when the man in black came screaming out of the rocky cleft. Ryker stepped in front of Mrs. MacLaren, shielding her as best he could. For once the mighty MacTavish retreated to his haunches, his bark replaced with a questioning whine.

Wild-eyed and looking over his shoulder, the stranger tore past waving and firing his pistol in the air Then without slowing his pace, he crashed through the surrounding terrain and disappeared. What had so unnerved this hardened mercenary?

At the snarling and a bloodcurdling scream, Ryker, Una, and MacTavish turned in unison. A white mountain lion stood at the mouth of the canyon.

****

Jim neared the bootlegger's territory, and the hair on at the nape of his neck stood erect as he slowed his pace to watch for sentries. The dappled sunlight and the song of a meadowlark belied the seriousness of his circumstances.

Cupping his hands at the sides of his mouth, he gave a remembered birdcall to indicate he was friendly. He hadn't been out to the *soda shop* in a long while. Hopefully the signal hadn't been changed and he wouldn't be mistaken for a Revenue agent and shot.

More people were moving to the frontier, including

the Women's Christian Temperance Union. Stiffer laws, and increased efforts to destroy home distilleries, had already begun. Locking up or shooting the participants would follow. The government wanted vengeance for not receiving taxes due on the products sold.

A man cradling a rifle stepped out of the trees, startling Jim. Then recognition brightened the man's eyes, and he motioned for Jim to follow. Farther into the woods, the trail became vague, and the forest closed in around them. After fifty yards, subdued voices could be heard.

"Look who's come to call." The man with the rifle led Jim over to three men sitting around a low burning fire.

"Bless my eyes, if it ain't Whiskey Jim." The oldest man in the group rose from the stump upon which he perched. Stooped and bewhiskered, he extended his hand and ambled closer with a noticeable limp.

"Howdy, Cletus." Jim took the proffered hand, and his own was vigorously pumped up and down.

"How are you and the boys doing? I was surprised to see Harlan in town the other day." Jim liberated his hand and glanced around. Positioned off to one side, hides from a variety of animals were stretched on frames to dry and sell to help make ends meet. Times were tough for his old friends.

"Ran low on tobaccie and coffee," Cletus said. "Two things we can't come by natural."

"I sure wish you'd consider turning toward more legitimate work. I'm always glad to help make that happen for you. With more people moving in, the

Federal boys aren't far behind. I'm concerned for your welfare."

"We talk about such notions—occasionally. But we're free spirits—who love strong spirits." Cletus laughed at his own joke. "Can't see any of us livin' in town being told what to do and when to do it."

"I understand. Just wanted you to be aware the offer still stands."

"Grab a stump, Whiskey Jim," another man offered. "We got an antelope roast about done on the spit, and it's a beggin' to be eaten."

To refuse such hospitality would be the epitome of rudeness, so Jim sauntered over and sat. There was a period in his life when he spent a good amount of time out here. He'd been top notch at running whiskey, hence his name. In an attempt to make ends meet and get ahead, he'd also spent a fair amount of time hunting for gold and silver.

As the jug came around, he stared at the flames. The mining had paid-off big time, and he'd drifted away from concocting the devil's brew he now swallowed.

Brimming with newfound confidence and a pocket full of silver, he'd dared to ask Sofia for her hand in marriage, and she'd taught him to read and write. From then on, keeping her safe and far away from this type of environment became a priority, which meant amicably breaking ties with these men.

He'd offered each of them a good paying job overseeing different aspects of his mining operation. But just like now, they'd flat-out refused while never begrudging him his success.

When Sofia passed away, he'd been devastated.

Still was. Unseen for nearly six months, when he finally went to town, unshaven and dressed in clothes he'd worn for weeks, no one recognized him as James Henry Merriman. He'd became Whiskey Jim again.

"Who'd you say the donkey was for?" Cletus's question cut through Jim's reminiscing, and he snapped back to the present.

"I don't believe I told Harlan."

"That burro's been a good worker, so we want her to have a good home."

In a new corral attached to the old cabin, whiskey could see the gray donkey he intended to purchase. "Why are you willing to sell her?"

"The twins jacks she birthed after we got her are growed up, and they don't behave as well when she's around. They get rowdy. If you get my drift."

"Well, you can rest easy. Where your donkey is going, she'll be properly cared for by the woman who owns the land."

"That eases my mind. Bet you're talking about the goat farmer up north of here. I seen you cutting through her property a time or two."

Not much of what happened nearby escaped the attention of these old timers. "As a matter of fact, you're correct. She's a good friend and needs to be treated as such."

"Wouldn't have things any other way." Jim took Cletus at his word. He'd never known him to treat a woman poorly.

Conversation came to a halt when Jim was handed a tin plate holding boiled corn-on-the-cob and slices of antelope roast full of flavor and tasting mighty fine. The squirrels and blue jays cautiously drew near waiting for scraps, and the camp hounds sat even closer eyes wide with hope. Eating Nature's bounty out of doors seemed natural and time honored. Jim relaxed and ate his fill.

When everyone finished, the man who'd offered up the grub grabbed a stick from the coals and lit up a cigar, and Jim rose to make the transaction and take his leave.

As they went to collect the jenny, he realized he should have asked Mrs. MacLaren for a halter. Cletus would have one but expect money in exchange—he didn't mind, he'd cover the expense. Besides, they'd wrapped up and gifted him several antelope steaks to take home. A generous offering.

Chapter Eight

"You see the critter too, right?"

"Aye," Una confessed. "But I'm not sure I'd admit such to anybody but you."

Mr. Jim had told Una the tale of the white panther but she had never seen the mythical mountain lion—until now. Magnificent and terrifying, a fire within set his yellow eyes to glowing, and the big cat exuded power while remaining ethereal.

As if assured the intruder was gone, the creature calmly ascended to the top of Cougar Rock and standing tall he gave another piercing scream. Then his image blurred, fading to smoke and mist and nothing.

"I won't tell if you won't," Ryker reassured. "I'm glad he scared off that bone hunter though. Maybe Dax won't come back."

"That would make your poking around all the easier, which I'm still dead set against."

"Aren't you at least curious to look at the relics?"

She was curious about a lot of things, like what it would be like to kiss this handsome rascal who had stepped in front of her when the bullets started flying. But that hardly meant she should.

"No, I'm not. Nothing good will come of the artifacts being disturbed."

"You could be right. So far, it's been a painful experience." Ryker glanced over his shoulder and grimaced.

"Good gracious, have you been shot?" How could she not have noticed Mr. Landry was injured and bleeding.

"No. A piece of rock tore loose when a bullet hit the cave wall. I think it's stuck in my shoulder."

"Come to the cabin. Quickly."

Without a second thought she'd invited him in to tend his wound. He didn't hesitate—but perhaps she should have. He was the first man to set foot inside her home since Hamish had died.

He sat by the woodstove as she gathered the emergency supplies kept in a small trunk by the front door. Other than Kathleen, no one came for a proper visit, so seeing anyone in her house, especially a man, was unfamiliar and startling. Yet also rather comforting. Another heartbeat in the house created energy. And MacTavish stood guard at the doorway, ready to spring into action at the first hint of trouble.

Ryker Landry glanced up and caught her staring. He had a winsome face, his eyes often merry with mischief as when they'd first met and he tried to sweet talk her into letting him dig around on her property.

Setting the kit and a bundle of clean rags on a small raw wood table, she shifted her focus to the task at hand. "You'll need to unbutton your shirt and slide the material down off your shoulder."

Wincing, he struggled to follow her request.

"Here, let me help." She eased the material over the wound, careful not to snag the fabric on the rough pointy rock protruding through the skin. Ryker's broad shoulders with well-defined muscles, stirred an interest deep inside her. "It's bleeding less now. A good sign."

"Bleeding less but hurting more. Just pull the dang thing out, will you."

"You'd be wise to speak more genteel to the woman about to do just that."

"I'm sorry. My words came out more unharmonious then intended."

"Apology accepted." Examining the situation, Una noted the stone splinter appeared unstable with a crack in the middle. "I'm afraid slowly and carefully might be a wiser approach, unless you want to risk leaving a piece in the wound. Here, bite on this." She handed him a wooden spoon from the utensil crock in the kitchen. Barely giving him time to place the handle crossways in his mouth, she began.

Steadying the skin around the wound with her left hand, she used the other to carefully work the stubborn object free. "It's out. The wound is deep but clean, I don't think the shard hit the bone."

Mr. Landry snatched the spoon from his mouth, inhaled a deep breath and then blew it out as if relieved the procedure was over.

Her flash of sympathy for his pain faded. After all, he'd gotten injured trespassing on her land after she told him not to go exploring. "This is what you get for going against the will of the land. I told you the cave and the area are sacred, and the spirits within were not to be provoked."

"Yes, so you've said. And real or fanciful, the white cougar didn't like us disturbing the canyon."

"*His* canyon, and I dare say he did appear ferociously annoyed. Here." She handed him the bloody piece of rock. "A keepsake of your misadventure."

"The shape is nearly a perfect arrowhead."

"More proof the native spirits are present. By the way, who was the man who ran off, and what started all the commotion?"

Mr. Landry's answer was slow in coming. Was he wrestling with how much to tell her, or deciding on which lie she would most likely swallow? "His name is Dax Thompson. He's searching for the same artifact I came to find. Only he doesn't care who he hurts or kills in order to get paid."

"His bad intentions don't make your reason for being here any less wrong." Searching through the supplies, she retrieved a bottle containing a brew of marigold, marshmallow plant, and coneflower. Pouring the liquid onto a cloth, she pressed the antiseptic concoction deep to the wound.

Mr. Landry stifled a groan of pain along with any reply.

Tugging the shirt lower on his back to accommodate wrapping the wound, a set of scars were revealed. "Oh mercy, your poor back." She hadn't meant to speak. His past or how he had come to receive marks from a lash was none of her business. She said no more and finished covering the newest injury added to his collection.

As he gained his feet, he slid his shirt into place obscuring not only the bandage but his history. Then he turned to face her. "Traveling the world can enrich your mind, but it's not always easy on your body."

"Wisdom earned the hard way. I didn't mean to pry."

Stepping into the kitchen area, she retrieved the jar of precious wound salve from the shelf. "Be sure to change the bandage every day. Keep the wound open, healing must come from the inside out." She offered these instructions over her shoulder as she transferred two spoonsful of the concoction into a small Mason jar. "If the wound becomes angry, put this around the edges." Screwing the lid down tight, she returned to his side, and handed him the glass container.

Holding the jar to the sunlight slanting in through the window, he furrowed his brow and scrutinized the contents.

"It's not pretty and smells to high Heaven, but the potion has been of great help around here saving many a goat who tangled with a snake or a sharp broken branch.

"Thank you. I appreciate your kindness. I'm sure I can find somebody around town to help me do as you've instructed."

By his tone, the possibility sounded doubtful. Cañon City wasn't always kind to strangers or loners. Since she'd become a widow, several of the married ladies treated her unkindly. Kate said they feared she might turn the heads of the male population, even the married ones. The women needn't have worried. There was freedom in being on her own. She was not seeking male companionship to complicate her life. The quickening of her heartbeat when she looked at Ryker indicated she was lying. If she tried, could she capture Ryker's attention?

"Come by tomorrow mid-morning and I'll help you," she relented. This way she could keep an eye on his comings and goings, and make sure he stayed out of the cave. Full of himself, he grinned as if believing his charm had won her over.

"I'd do the same for any wounded animal."

****

Remembering how they met, Mrs. MacLaren's offer was the last thing Ryker expected. Was he making progress getting on her good side? Maybe there was hope after all of laying his hands on the relics. Before he could come up with a line of conversation to further ingratiate himself to her, Wallace began to bray and the sound of casual whistling could be heard.

As if she forgot he was there, she hurried out the front door, MacTavish at her heels. Jar in hand, Ryker followed.

Leading a donkey even bigger than Wallace, a man materialized out of the south woods. Ryker stopped short his hand on the butt of his holstered weapon. Good thing he'd reloaded after the shootout with Dax.

"Don't be alarmed." Mrs. MacLaren waved him aside. "He's a friend."

It was the scraggly fellow Ryker had seen camped at the mouth of the cave. As he approached, wariness sharpened the old man's features, and he appeared less congenial and more intimidating.

"Oh Mr. Jim, she's beautiful." Mrs. MacLaren eased closer to examine the animal being led.

Ryker found the term rather a stretch being applied to a shaggy gray donkey, but he thought better of saying so.

"What's her name?"

Whiskey Jim chuckled. "I plumb forgot to ask."

"I shall call her The Countess, after Winifred Countess of Nithsdale." She stroked the long ears, the attention well received. "May you be as stalwart, clever, and long-lived as your namesake. I can hardly wait for you to meet Sir William Wallace."

Ryker wondered if Mrs. MacLaren often had these flights of fancy. Whiskey Jim beamed affectionately at the woman, convincing him this type of nonsensical talk was not unusual.

A mismatched group, they walked to the fence where the brown donkey worried the rails and let loose with an even more exuberant heehaw.

The ears on the gray jenny perked up, and she carried herself more erect and light-footed as if showing off for the gelding, who apparently found her beguiling.

"Oh, just look. Wallace is already taken with her. What wonderful companions they shall make. The pair will be useful pulling the sleigh or the open market wagon. She comes at a great price to my purse and my heart but is worth every penny."

Ryker held up the bottle of ointment. "Thank you for tending my wound. I'll take you up on having another go at torturing me tomorrow." He nodded a goodbye. "I'd better head out."

A curious look passed between Whiskey Jim and Mrs. MacLaren. "You're welcome to make camp with me by the cave," the older man offered.

Ryker wasn't about to pass up a chance to stay near the canyon where he could guard the treasure from the likes of Dax Thompson. Oddly this urge to protect was almost as strong as the urge to dig.

****

Ryker tended to his horse and threw out a bedroll. His shoulder ached, but the pain was bearable. He would have been in dire straits if not for Mrs. MacLaren's ministrations.

Without complaint, he gathered wood for the fire, and hauled water in the buckets Whiskey Jim provided.

He'd explained about the altercation with Dax and felt a modicum of responsibility for the discombobulation of the older man's camp.

When evening drew nigh, Ryker was ready for supper and all the quiet time he could get.

Whiskey Jim rummaged in his pack, and retrieved antelope meat, a turnip, and wild onions. Before long, the stew he whipped up began to simmer and Ryker threw hardtack on top to commence soaking. A man couldn't have asked for a better meal.

In the stillness following their meal, the temperature dropped swiftly. Night sounds could be heard in the nearby woods, while they sat hunched around the fire pit taking turns tossing on just enough wood to keep the coals alive.

Ryker suspected the vagabond image Whiskey Jim portrayed, disguised a much more complex man housing a fund of local knowledge. Since darkness often inspired talk not to be uttered in the light of day, he decided to start the conversation.

"You been around these parts long?"

"Most of my life."

"I reckon you staying put gives credence to a place."

"Either that or to a man's laziness to move on. Where do you hail from?"

"Born in Kentucky, but I've set my foot down in many a country."

"I figured you had the wanderlust in you. Not being the type to settle down, you'd best keep clear of Mrs. MacLaren. I'd not like to see her feelings trifled with by a drifter."

"That's strong talk."

"Glad you picked up on that. She's got enough troubles without contending with the likes of you."

"You mean like the cattlemen? They aren't shy about their feelings toward her, or clandestine about their ploys to make her life miserable."

"You're the one rigged the broken fence closed the night the goats got out"

"Maybe."

"One good deed won't make up for you hanging around here uninvited."

"Didn't expect that it would."

"Did you ever sleep in the cave?"

"Once, for a short time and never again. There's something not right in there."

"Or maybe there's something not right in you."

Ryker vigorously tossed a piece of wood on the fire. Sparks flew into the night sky—a spark of annoyance flared up in his belly. The old man's words hit close to home. Was he doing the right thing? Usually not a concern and not a welcome complication, Ryker had begun to question his motives on this undertaking. The woman was the cause, the one he'd just been asked to—no threatened to—avoid. "For an old man you seem quick to hand out words likely to start an altercation."

"Actually, I'm more interested in keeping things peaceable around here. There're legends living in the shadows of Break Heart Canyon. Traditional stories easily lost. When they are, the world loses a tiny connection to the past which affects all of us."

"Who died and made you keeper of the land?"

"My family set foot here many generations ago, I grew up with the stories. The legends shouldn't be wiped out as easily as the tribes who once roamed this territory."

"What tribe lived here?"

"Mostly the Ute people."

This tallied with what Mr. Cockrell had told Ryker. One more detail indicating he was looking for the prize in the correct place. "Then you've obviously heard about the breastplate." No use tiptoeing around the subject. Maybe he could persuade Whiskey Jim to see his side. "Shouldn't the ancient handiwork be appreciated by the world?"

"Appreciated? You mean used to bolster the ego of men who haven't set foot west of the Mississippi. Men who don't know or care anything about the people who created what you've come for or what true value it once held."

"Men buy paintings, racehorses, houses, any number of things to admire and show their wealth."

"But those things were made to be sold or traded. The breastplate was made to be honored."

The old man's attitude didn't sound encouraging, but he couldn't guard the cave every minute of every day, and one way or another, Ryker had to get his hands on the object before Dax Thompson found it first.

"It's cursed, you know."

Ha. Ryker had heard that line before. There was hardly a pirate's treasure, jeweled necklace, or Egyptian grave that didn't come with a curse. Maybe he could find a way around the curse if he knew what it entailed. "How did the curse come about?"

Being his turn, Jim threw another log on the fire. In the flair of light, the old man's eyes gleamed, but with what—humor, anger, madness? "I'll tell you what I can, but the knowledge comes at a price"

****

Una crawled into bed and blew out the nearby candle.

What a lively day filled with extraordinary events. The Countess seemed happy in her new home. Or maybe the nice grass hay and tidbit of sweet feed she'd been given this evening was to her liking. The donkey didn't appear mistreated but was a bit underweight.

Wallace was smitten with her. Whenever he stood beside her, you could almost see little hearts and flowers spiraling off his long-eared head.

With a sigh, Una fluffed her pillow and flopped over onto one side. Although tired to the bone, sleep wouldn't come. The knowledge Mr. Jim and Mr. Landry were not far away should be a comfort to her rather than enlivening her senses. Since first encountering Mr. Landry, a restlessness ate away at her, forcing Una to admit she was lonely.

When left alone for long periods of time, she grew accustomed to the solitude with having only the animals for company. She kept busy with the farm and carding and spinning and dying and knitting. She was content, fostering few expectations. But with the recent flurry of activity, a long-forgotten excitement came alive within her. Something she had worked hard to ignore and bury along with Hamish.

And now there was the coming eclipse, a monumental convergence. Universal in scope, the occurrence also seemed eminent in her personal world, heralding a wondrous change, but of what type—peaceful or calamitous? Something told her to expect both.

Una yawned and stared into the darkness. Her brain churned with too many thoughts, too many worries, too many circumstances with which she alone must deal. Some days she wanted to run away from it all. If she'd had the energy, she would get up, put on a pair of sturdy boots, and wrapped in her chemise and shawl, with her hair set free, she would bound through the tall grass like a whitetail deer. She'd run and run and run…

Chapter Nine

Ryker knew the old man was playing him, but his interest being piqued, he went along with the annoying nonsense. "What's the price for the information?"

"The cost is different for everyone."

"Meaning?"

"Meaning each man carries his own debt in the world, an individual karmic coinage, so to speak."

"Each man also carries his own moral compass, they aren't all set on due north."

"True enough. Tonight, let's say the fee is your time and consideration."

That seemed harmless enough. "I'm in." Ryker didn't expect listening to these myths and fables would be of much help. Yet one never knew where a nugget of truth might be buried.

With a nod of agreement, Whiskey hunkered down and began spinning his tale.

"When the mountains erupted and tore a path down the middle of this country, there was power and magic in the birthing. The once flat horizon turned into these formidable stone monuments, reaching for the heavens. Then, having journeyed across the causeway from another land, the people arrived.

"The ancient ones recognized the magic and formed a kinship with the Earth—the likes of which we will never understand. But over thousands of years and with each new generation, the miraculous connection faded and the people divided into tribes. The magic was abandoned or used to turn brother against brother. Taking refuge, the spirit of what was now lives in the deserts and mountains and caves and canyons—places people tend to avoid. Pieces of the magic remain here. Your intentions will disturb what should remain at peace."

Ryker shifted his gaze toward Break Heart Canyon. Beyond their circle of light, the view faded to pitch black. The night sounds seemed louder than before, and although the fire crackled with warmth, a chill slid down his spine. He ignored the feeling. So far nothing he'd heard convinced him to alter his plans. "That's quite the story."

Whiskey Jim shrugged. "Stories become myth, and myth becomes legend.

"What about the artifact, and the white cougar?"

"Ah, your mercenary objective, and the guardian of the canyon. Hang on, we'll get there eventually. Have you someplace you'd rather be?"

Ryker envisioned Mrs. MacLaren. Was she awake? She sure had been excited about the donkey. Happiness had shone in her face—sunlight couldn't have warmed him more. And her red hair intrigued him, different, special, full of the fire for life.

"Someplace besides over there." Whiskey Jim cautioned. "You don't seem the settling down type. She deserves better than to be someone's passing fancy."

"Seems such a choice would be up to her."

"A given, of course. I just don't want to see her get her heart broken again. There may be no mending the wound a second time around."

"Well, this *is* Break Heart Canyon." His words came out flippant and unfeeling when he had no intentions of hurting the woman. He'd make sure to get permission to take what he wanted—if not from the land, at least from her.

"Another of her heartaches, don't need to be added to an already sad tale."

"What happened the first time? To the MacLaren woman, I mean."

"That's not for me to say."

"According to town gossip, when her husband died two years ago, she claimed the cattlemen were responsible for his death. They claim they weren't. The sheriff sided with the cattlemen."

"Then you heard the gist of it."

"Whose side are you on."

"I'm generally on the side of *to each his own*. But when one man's path cuts across another's with dire consequences, not getting involved becomes almost impossible. The cattlemen have overstepped their rights, unfortunately important people in this county have crossed those lines with them. They deserve a comeuppance."

Whiskey Jim's last words were said with chilling determination.

"You talk pretty brave for a down on his luck town-character. Who are you really?"

Whiskey gave a snort of amused. "Like you, I wear many hats. I doubt you are a calloused mercenary. You may need money, but it's the adventure you seek. And your hesitation in robbing the dead will save you."

"You'd be surprised at what I'm willing to do—and have done.

"Possibly. Besides it's what your capable of becoming that counts. If you sleep in the cave, you will know your true self."

"Oooh no. You won't catch me sleeping in there. Whether or not there's magic or even a curse dwelling in the depths of the cave, I'm not going in there for any reason other than to finish the job I'm being paid to do." Ryker toyed with a stick, marking random patterns in the soil at his feet.

He'd hoped listening to the old man might reveal new information. So far, the history lesson hadn't been helpful, and neither had he won the old man over to his way of thinking by fawning interest. "What about the white cougar and the way the canyon got its name."

"The tale is rather Shakespearian."

This reference caught Ryker's attention—another indication Whiskey Jim was an educated man. What a curious fellow.

"The story begins with the predecessors of the Ute Indians, ancient men who lived in these canyons thousands of years ago. Their history was passed down by word of mouth.

"In more recent times, 1834 to be exact, my grandfather became acquainted with the decedents of the ancients. During the early fur-trade era, Grandpa fancied himself an explorer, and I guess he was as the frontier had yet to be conquered. Grandma doggedly followed her man, happy to be wherever he led as long as they could be together."

"Grandpa felt at home with the native people, and he gained much from them including their love of the land and knowledge of how to survive in the wilderness. He also realized what damage and suffering the opening of the West would cause them.

"One year he travelled back to Washington to stop the mistreatment, and to fight for their rights. The tribe honored him for his attempts to help, and he became family. That's when he heard the legend of Break Heart Canyon. A tale of life and death, and love and hate. But mostly a story of remorse."

Oh geez. Things were turning philosophical. Being pretty much a captive audience, Ryker let the man ramble on.

"We can't help the hand we're dealt, but there are always choices. Making the wrong one, or not having the courage to make one at all, can lead to regret. And regret is the saddest human foible over which we lament at the hour of our death."

Tarnation, now things were really getting into territory he'd rather not explore tonight, or any time. "Speaking of regret, I'm beginning to feel a great amount for agreeing to listen to this long, long story."

Jim laughed and slapped one knee. "I do tend to get carried away. Most folks around here were brought up hearing a good portion of what I'm telling you, so I don't often get the chance to recount my tale in a more dramatic fashion."

The older man leaned forward conspiratorially. "Actually, no one has heard the entire story. Normally I wouldn't reveal any of this to a stranger. No sir, the idea wouldn't even cross my mind. But I have a feeling you were sent here for more than mercenary gains."

"So now you're a fortune teller too."

"No, but I am a pretty good judge of character."

"I thought I was a no-account travelling man, not worthy of the lady whose land upon which we squat."

"That's who you are now. But you haven't slept in the cave."

"Back to that old song. Ain't gonna happen, old man. Now get on with your story before I fall asleep right here."

"All right, all right. Being part of the Bone Wars, you obviously heard about the monsters who once roamed the earth. The ancient unnamed tribes also knew they once existed. The relic you seek is older than you may have been told. Endowed by rituals lost for all time, your employer may not know the power the breastplate holds.

"The spirit of the canyon is held within the petrified teeth, quills, and earth paints. And the cave protects the breastplate, as well as what was left of the shaman and the bones of the last chief of this unknown tribe. To disturb any of what is hidden inside may be catastrophic. No one knows because no one dares to find out."

"So you're telling me all this in hopes of persuading me to stop searching for the artifact."

"No. I'm telling you all this so you realize what you're facing if you remove the sacred objects."

"I already know where it is."

"Yes, I saw where you broke through into the burial chamber."

"And you patched the hole." Not wishing to speak further about what he had or had not been up to, and as the story seemed to be on intermission, he changed the subject.

"Nice of you to find a donkey for Mrs. MacLaren. Why'd you charge her so much?

"I charged her a fair price. She's the kind of

woman who wouldn't accept charity, wants to pay her own way."

Maybe that was why she'd sold the sparkly rock. The one stashed in his haversack. "After the excitement wore off from getting the animal, she appeared a bit pale."

"Aye, she did. Couldn't have anything to do with getting caught in the crossfire of your personal shenanigans I suppose."

More guilt shoveled his way. Ryker pushed the feeling aside. He was trying to make his own way too, and in any war, including the Bone Wars, the innocent were often the worse for the machinations of others. Besides, he hadn't taken on this work to fight for noble causes.

Gaining his feet, Ryker stretched then stepped away from the fire and into the brush to relieve himself. An owl hooted, and as the moon rose higher in a cloudless sky casting shadows, which seemed to slink about in the far trees, the white cougar came to mind.

When Ryker reclaimed his stump by the fire, Whiskey Jim sat smoking a pipe, appearing the picture of contentment. Ryker couldn't remember the last time he felt a sense of serenity. The inner voice driving him demanded he *keep searching, keep moving on*. Lately the lure of adventure had lost a bit of luster, and he answered the call more out of habit than excitement.

As he sat in the night, his wound aching, he felt old—well maybe not old, but definitely older. So far, this venture was not living up to his expectations. He'd been shot at, had his shoulder pierced near to the bone, had his days turned into nights, and had spent his hard-earned cash on a useless object belonging to a woman he hardly knew. Removing his hat, he ran one hand through his hair as if doing so might clear his thinking. Instead, it made him angry. He jammed his hat back into place—he was getting soft.

Whiskey Jim enjoyed another few drags on his pipe before tapping out the ash on a nearby rock. "It's getting late. Guess I'll turn in."

What the heck. The man wasn't going to finish telling the elaborate fairytale he'd been jawing about half the night. Much to his vexation, Ryker was actually anticipating hearing more about the fable. "If you're too old and tired to finish what you started, that's all right by me."

Whiskey Jim grinned, knowing he'd hooked Ryker's interest. "Where was I in the retelling of this yarn of long ago?"

"The part where you'd rather I didn't get my hands on the artifact, and there are human bones in there too."

"Ah, yes. The remains of two men. Once friends, they died as enemies. The skeleton belongs to the chief of the ancient people. The jumble of white bones is that of the shaman. His standing in the hierarchy of the clan was equal to the chief's.

"Together, the two leaders balanced one another, and the group thrived. Then the chief's daughter wished to marry a warrior her father deemed unsuitable, and the chief forbade the marriage. Using his dream spells to divine the future, the shaman discovered one thing kept from the father—the daughter was with child. If the secret came to light, the girl would be driven from the society and the young man killed. Running away together was the young couple's only chance.

"Revealing the plan to no one, the shaman arranged

for their escape. He alone protected the secrets of the canyon, including the only safe passage through the towering unforgiving rocks."

Ryker sat up straighter. Finally, a bit of useful information. "Do you remember the path? Where is the exit? What's on the other side?"

Whiskey Jim sighed and shook his head as if discerning Ryker's renewed interest in the story was self-serving. "That's not information I'm at liberty to share, and is not the point of the legend. When the escape came to light, the chief was furious. He sought the shaman and found him sitting before a fire with his eyes closed as he contemplated the netherworld. The chief called him out, but the shaman wouldn't answer, already foreseeing his fate.

"Blinded by rage, the chief struck a mighty blow with his war ax to the shaman's head, killing him instantly. The shaman's body turned to white smoke, forming what appeared to be a great cat. Sworn even in death to protect the mountains, the image drifted up into the hills. Nothing remained where the elder sat except his bones—white and picked clean as if they had been there for many years."

"You mean all these centuries later, people believe his spirit is hanging out up there on Cougar Rock?"

"You tell me? Did you not see him?"

"I saw…something. In all the excitement and being injured and all, it's hard to say for sure." He was reluctant to confess he'd seen the ghost cat, but he admitted he was curious as to whether or not the warrior and his woman survived the journey though the canyon. "Did the young lovers get away."

"Remaining full of fury, the chief demanded his

bravest tribesmen find his daughter and bring the young man back to be killed. None of the search party returned, and now their families mourned too.

"The people of the clan became disillusioned and angry. Their chief had taken their shaman/medicine man from them and sent their kin to perish in the cruel depths of the canyon. Many left to form their own tribes. Others demanded payment for such treatment.

"On the verge of madness, the chief ignored their plight. He gathered the Shaman's bones and sacred flute, and wearing the breastplate you covet, he took these items to the cave never to be seen outside again. Haunted by having killed his childhood friend whom he had loved as a brother, and believing his daughter had died a horrible death in the unforgiving towering rocks, his mind turned dark as the cave. For many nights, frightful sounds came from the black opening warning man and beast to stay away."

A large ember exploded in the center of the campfire, sending a ball of fire straight for Ryker. He jumped at the sound then swatted away the flaming cinder clinging to and burning a hole in his pants leg. This story was making him jumpy as a March hare. He crushed the smoldering chunk of bark beneath his boot, but the distraction didn't cool his desire to hear more.

"Did the chief dig out the room at the back of the cave?" Not looking up and pretending disinterest, he casually hinted for Whiskey to continue.

"Yes—it became his tomb. After many weeks of wailing and chaos, there came several days of total quiet, and one foolishly brave soul crept inside to see what had happened. He could barely conceive of what was revealed. Their chief was dead, his face contorted into a mask of terror. To gaze upon the death grimace made one's heart falter. The man, who had taken but one quick peek, became weak and was never the same. Other foolish attempts ended in even more horrific results, and the room was walled up to prevent anyone else from entering."

"But what about the breastplate?"

"Touching the petrified teeth on the relic left horrible burns never to heal on the hands and fingers of the few who sought the power. To dare to hold the Shaman's flute caused blindness and madness and the turning of one's bones to dust.

"The chief and the shaman once bound together in life by love and loyalty, were separated by hate and revenge. Now as they lay side by side, they do not rest in peace, and are better left alone."

A coyote howled, sending a chill down Ryker's spine. The perfect ending to this cautionary tale. Of all the stories he heard of curses and sorcery, this one ranked right up there with the best.

****

Una continued to toss and turn. She knew Wallace and The Countess guarded the goats, still the yipping of the coyotes fueled her unrest.

Thoughts of Mr. Landry sleeping nearby didn't help either. When she knew not where he was or what he was up to, she could avoid picturing the rogue's warm brown eyes and sensuous mouth—a mouth inclined toward humor.

Now she couldn't help but picture him stretched out by the campfire near the cave. Would lying beside him be as arousing as she imagined? His mere existence robbed her not only of her slumber, but of her good senses.

When he was around, her breathing became difficult, as if a long-forgotten sensation crowded the air out of her chest, making her lightheaded. The effect was frightful and exciting, and she questioned her ability to keep resisting such emotions. Thank goodness he wouldn't be interrupting her life for long.

Why did he have to show up now when she already had more than enough concerns?The cattlemen were a persistent lot, they wouldn't give up on their attempts to drive her off, and with the Countess added to the list of animals who needed food when snow covered the pastures, would there be enough hay? Would the Arkansas river flood, or the creek dry up and become mud?

Like a chicken with a bowl of cracked corn, worry pecked, pecked, pecked at her mood and her brain. But she must survive through the end of 1878 to fulfill her homestead requirements. Then if she physically moved on, she would not forfeit the land she owned free and clear.

She could do it. She had to—or lose everything. But she was weary, being alone meant no one with whom to share the burden of worry and decision making. Here was another part of her life harder since losing Hamish.

Hamish... The fleeting pleasure she felt for Mr. Landry carried a smattering of guilt as if she were cheating on her husband dead and gone. She had known Hamish nearly all her life, they had grown up together, seemingly destined to be husband and wife. She'd only known Mr. Landry a matter of minutes. He was the great unknown, unexpected and exciting—and a mercenary—practically an outlaw. He would have even less concern for her heart then he showed for the artifacts he hunted for profit.

Chapter Ten

The next morning, when Ryker crawled out of his bedroll, Whiskey Jim was gone.

Prodding the coals in the firepit back into life, he heated up the day-old coffee in the pot kindly left behind. Whisky Jim was an unusual man, and the tale he told last night had been even more strange.

Lost in thought, trying to separate fact from fiction, Ryker watched steam rising from the spout of the enameled pot. If he didn't know better, he'd declare the last twenty-four hours, beginning with Dex Thompson shooting at him, had been a dream.

Reaching for the coffee pot, pain shot through Ryker's shoulder, a reminder the fight had been real enough. Sampling the bitter brew quickly revived him and he retrieved a packet of hardtack and munched away as he continued contemplating recent events.

Coming to Break Heart Canyon felt like crossing a barrier where what was real hovered on the edge of what could be or what once was. The concept wasn't so crazy. There were many unseen lines in the world, and while they were invisible, they did not go unfelt, and they demanded respect.

The first time he'd crossed the Equator, he'd been a young wide-eyed deckhand on a merchant ship heading for Brazil. Along with the rest of the apprentice seafarers, he'd been made to pay homage to King

Neptune in a line crossing ceremony—a jovial yet harsh initiation. And when he'd straddled the Equator in Africa, water swirled clockwise to the north of him, anticlockwise to the south—in the exact middle, nothing swirled at all. There were rules governing the Earth—longitudes and latitudes, the tropic of Cancer, the tropic of Capricorn. Why not a line here marking properties he couldn't explain.

Sensing movement, Ryker jumped to his feet—his teeth clenched at the sudden return of pain. MacTavish appeared first, loping in his direction, tongue lolling. Then Mrs. MacLaren came into view. As she moved from shadow to light, her braid of red captured the sunlight. He delighted in watching her approach.

Tall and willowy and wrapped in her plaid shawl of blues and greens, she seemed one with the land. A small kid goat bounced and gamboled along in her wake. As a breeze ruffled the stray strands of her hair, he longed to wrap them around his fingers or grasp the astonishing red mane by the handful to draw her close for a stolen kiss.

When she drew near, she stopped short as if startled by the intensity of his observance. "Good morning, fair damsel." Ryker jested, trying to act casual.

"I've come to tend your wound." She held up the basket she carried, then she advanced and set the wicker upon one of the stumps near the campfire. Her matter-of-fact statement held no congeniality, and the warmth he'd felt in her yesterday had disappeared. He wondered what had changed.

****

"And who's this?"

Una stood in silence as Mr. Landry reached down and patted the playful kid sucking on the tail of her shawl.

Why was she drawn to the sound of his voice and the kindness he showed her animals? Such affectations didn't matter and would lead to no good.

"MacTavish, mind the goat." Heeding her command, the dog gently nudged the rambunctious baby off to the side. Then he guarded, and by means of entertainment, kept the energetic bit of fuzz and fluff out of their way.

The cheeky little goat tried headbutting the dog, and the antics of the little Angora eased her out of her downhearted mood. "The poor bairn had a rough beginning. For a fortnight I feared she wouldna make it, but as you can tell from her shenanigans, she's doing much better."

"Thanks to you, I'm feeling better too."

She shifted her gaze back to Mr. Landry and stifled a gasp of surprise. He'd removed his hat, jacket, and shirt in record time. Appropriate enough as she was to dress his shoulder. But she'd imagined seeing the shift from fully clothed to bare chested revealed slowly so she could adjust to the sight of his wide shoulders and nicely muscled torso. He stood tall, and casually ran one hand across the lite shadowing of hair accentuating the muscles of his chest and abdomen.

"Yes, you do appear quite healthy today."

The memory of him sitting in her kitchen had invaded her sleepless night. Which was partly the reason she had come to him rather than allowing him once more inside her home—an overly personal setting. The first time had been a mistake. No use making more disturbing recollections to haunt her long after he was gone. Loneliness and wishes for happiness were already in abundance in the cold dark corners come winter.

"Please, take a seat."

Unabashed at her perusal he sat. To recover a modicum of composure, she turned to organize the bandages and medicines.

Removing the old bandage, she tossed the bloody scrap into the firepit.

"The wound seems healthy. The only drainage is strong red blood. But you must keep the opening packed and covered so the healing will continue from the inside out."

"I'll certainly do my best," he promised.

"Where are you staying tonight?"

"I haven't decided. And thank you for letting me camp here last evening. With the eclipse tomorrow, most places in the town are standing room only. They doubled the rate at the hotel, so a few nights ago I vacated my room and spent the night at the livery with my horse. The stable got crowded too. The only folks sitting pretty are the Governor and his friends who have arrived to watch the event halfway up Pike's Peak. Their comfort and accommodations took priority."

"From the gray patch in the sky, they might be having snow up there."

"Ha, serves them right."

"You can't be meanin' that. After all the commotion, what a travesty if noothin' came of the grand show because a little cloud got in the way. Tis an event of a lifetime."

"Maybe so. And casting ill fortune on others never bodes well."

Ryker's last words gave her an inkling of hope he could still be persuaded not to disturb the artifact. "There's a saying what you wish for others will come back to you threefold. What do you wish for in the dead of night?" The words were out before she considered their invasive nature."

"I wish people would stay out of my business and let me do what I came here for."

"Of course, silly of me to ask." Why had she expected a reasonable answer? Dismayed and irritated at his response, she still took care to gently pack the wound.

"I've never looked beyond one day at a time," he added. "The future being hard to predict."

Now his words seemed contemplative and sincere, tinged with a bit of sadness. Wandering the world sounded a lonely business, an affliction which surely worsened with age.

The bright sunshine down here in the valley felt good, and she didn't intend for this stubborn man to dull the excitement the eclipse engendered. "I wonder what the animals will make of the event."

"I guess we'll have to wait and see. They could take a fit and run about scared and wild-eyed. Maybe I should be here with you when the eclipse takes place?"

She doubted anything of the kind would happen and didn't believe he thought so either. But his offer to share the experience pleased her greatly—even though she knew being near him was dangerous to her wildly beating heart and should be avoided without exception.

"I'd enjoy your company." She hadn't meant to sound so enthusiastic, and finished tying off the bandage, she patted her handy work a little too enthusiastically.

"Ouch. Is a sound beating part of the treatment?"

"For the likes of you, yes."

He gained his feet and turned toward her, and she laughed at his expression.

Realizing she was kidding, he also gave a burst of laughter and grabbed up his shirt. His gaze never left her face as he shrugged into the flannel and slid each button into place.

Her cheeks warmed as she watched the display, and no doubt her fair skin betrayed her without mercy. Oh bother, why was she attracted to this no-gooder? Heaven only knew what he'd done in the past if this was his idea of making a living in the here and now.

He'd already invaded her property and her thoughts, and now the effects of having him around were spreading from her mind to other highly sensitive parts of her body.

Fiddling with his hat, he glanced up at her through dark lashes she wished she had. "My staying here one more night would sure be a big help. Especially me being wounded and all."

Only MacTavish could have managed a more soulful expression.

No, no, no. She should say no. But the words, "*I suppose such an arrangement would be acceptable*" came out of her mouth instead. She didnae want him to leave.

"You're an angel of mercy in more ways than one. I appreciate your consideration."

Ignoring, yet secretly enjoying his flamboyant and ingratiating compliment, she finished repacking her basket. "I'll be getting on with my day then and leave you to your own devices. Come, MacTavish, and bring the wee one." There were plenty of chores to keep her busy and safely far away from the likes of Mr. Landry.

****

Observing Mrs. MacLaren take her leave was every bit as enjoyable as watching her approach. She slid the shawl from her shoulders and looped the wool around the handle of the basket swinging at her side.

With her free hand she captured and flung that tempting red braid back over her shoulder as if the plait had offended her—or as if she were disturbed by something or somebody. He hadn't missed the appealing blush on her cheeks as she'd watched him shrug into his shirt. He was winning her over.

After she'd disappeared from sight, Ryker lit a lantern and wandered into the cave. Giving him permission to stay until tomorrow was almost an invitation for him poke around. Did she fancy he would just sit and admire the view betwixt now and then?

Squeezing through the fissure to the back area, he studied the patch. Smashing open the handywork seemed the wrong move at present. He should try one more time to gain the help of Whiskey Jim and Mrs. MacLaren. Or what the heck, a little help from the Giant Powder Company would make short work of things once and for all. That image appealed to the reckless side of his nature.

Chapter Eleven

Una washed the last of the wild strawberries and blueberries and set them in the colander to drain. There were just enough for two decent size pies to celebrate tomorrow's eclipse. When MacTavish whined, she sacrificed one strawberry, tossing the treat to him which he caught midair. She swore he licked his chops and grinned.

Adding wood to the stove, she grabbed the salt, flour, lard, and her special ingredient—honey. How she loved her precious bees and the honey they provided.

Humming a little tune, she mixed and rolled out the dough. The afternoon was a special time to enjoy. Wallace and The Countess were free range on guard duty, and she was only pleasantly tired from cleaning the barn and picking the berries for the pies. And being too hot for hoeing and hauling, she had the perfect excuse for not weeding the herb garden today.

Although clouds remained tethered to Pike's Peak, the sunshine in her valley kept her spirits high. Or was seeing Mr. Landry the reason for the spring in her step and the happy tune buzzing around in her head. Oh fiddle-faddle, she smacked the ball of dough with the wooden rolling pin. She wished she'd never met the man.

Using her irritation, she rolled out her thinnest piecrust ever. While the pies baked, she gathered her drop spindle, carding paddles, and a basket of mohair roving.

Her old spinning wheel needed a part. Mr. Franks at the general store assured her he could order what she needed, if she were to pay upfront. Her brow furrowed. What a merry-go-round. She needed to sell her woolen items to make money and needed the part to make them more quickly. And if she used the ten dollars in reserve, she'd have to start all over saving up to buy back her sparkly rock. She loved that stone, and how it caught the morning sunlight—starting her day with a bit of magic.

Setting the spindle to twirling, her shoulders relaxed, and before long she got caught up in the soothing repetition of drawing out the fiber and watching in wonder as the wool roving transformed into yarn. The next step would be making two ply and setting the twist to use for knitting. Lots to do before the final product could be used.

She'd spent the spring planting beets and spinach, and nursing along the blueberry bushes. Little of these garden labors went for meals, she used these particular vegetables and fruit to dye her wool. Having playful colors with which to work added to the creativity of making the items and inspired sales.

When she sat happily spinning, time slipped away unnoticed, and before she knew it, the pastries smelled done. Protecting her hands with a thick towel, she removed the hot pies and placed each one on the windowsill. They needed to cool sufficiently before storing them in the pie keeper for the night.

Pleased with her accomplishment, she took a break from spinning to climb the hill and check on the beehives. A wind had swooped down the valley the other day, leaving one stack of hives listing.

****

Ryker collected the last of his meager belongings stored at an unreasonable rate in a smelly back room of the hotel/restaurant. His new plan was to prolong his stay on Mrs. MacLaren's property from one more night to indefinitely. Now as he crossed her farm from the far side, he checked out the area more closely. Like the woman, her homestead was a contrast of rough timber and soft valley. Mrs. MacLaren seemed a compassionate woman—with an underlying *don't screw with me kind of attitude*. He recalled how she'd stood up to the cattlemen in the general store, like the fluffy kid goat standing up to MacTavish. But the dog knew not to kill the goat. He wasn't so sure about the cattlemen. The world was full of real wolves.

He'd also seen her softer side when she cared for him following his injury. Sitting in the kitchen had eased not only the pain in his shoulder, but for a moment the loneliness he felt in his soul. Then as if she'd come to her senses, her demeanor had changed. A temporary setback, given enough time, he was sure he could win her over.

While his horse stopped to munch on prairie grass, Ryker searched the horizon and spotted Una up on the hill near the beehives. She had not given him permission to use her given name, but in his mind, he found the sound pleasing and to his liking.

This was the first time he'd seen her unbound hair—ginger red, streaked with burnished gold. Gold—from nuggets to necklaces, men had lost their good senses over the shine and feel of the prize. Was he

100

losing his good senses over this mere slip of a woman? Ridiculous. He wasn't about to fall prey to romantic drivel. He was here to use her to his advantage, not vice versa.

Other than when they were in his arms, Ryker rarely spent a lot of time pondering what women wanted. From Paris to Punjab, he'd enjoyed his share of dalliances. The ladies knew upfront he wouldn't stay long, and he knew they came to him only for what he bought them. A mutually agreed upon relationship—all parties duly satisfied. But he must tread lightly here. Mrs. MacLaren was different, certainly not the type to be distracted by shiny objects or faithless words of love.

And when all was said and done, would he stay or leave Colorado? The idea of leaving seemed to be slipping away like an unmoored boat drifting unnoticed toward the open sea. Mrs. MacLaren inspired a slower pace in him. A deeper awareness and appreciation of the land. And surprisingly, Whiskey Jim inspired thoughts of friendship. Had he seen enough of the world to last a lifetime?

This untamed burgeoning West did have its appeal—as did the woman he watched from afar. Una... Yes, he preferred thinking of her as Una, not Mrs. Somebody-else's. Again, why should he care?

"Staying here again tonight, are you?"

With a start, Ryker twisted in the saddle one hand on the butt of his revolver.

"Easy there, cowboy. It's just me." Not paying attention, he'd let Whiskey Jim sneak up on him. And allowing his horse to choose the easiest path, they'd wandered in the direction of Una's cabin.

That's what he got for succumbing to flights of

fancy. Complacency could be dangerous. Dax Thompson could have just as easily sneaked up on him. These surroundings were affecting his sensibilities, heightening some while softening others. Yes, softening, as if the rough edges had been filed off him. No good could come from such a change. Living could be hard, and a man had to be harder.

With a grumble of irritation at having been caught unaware, Ryker stepped down from his horse and walked beside Whiskey Jim. "Before you start with the questions or lectures, I have permission to be here. And you sure are out and about around here a lot yourself."

"Yes. I am."

"By the way, thanks for leaving the coffee this morning."

"Don't take it personal. I just didn't want to be the one to clean the pot."

As their path took them around the backside of Una's cabin, Ryker noted two pies sitting on the kitchen windowsill. One was blueberry.

Nose sniffing the air, a large fox spotted the pastry at the same time. Before Ryker or Whiskey could intercept the agile critter, the bold as brass interloper clambered onto the woodpile stacked alongside the cabin. Balanced on the top log, the critter reached one furry paw toward the forbidden treat.

Whooping and hollering, the men successfully scared away the wily thief, but one pie was left teetering on the edge. They'd never reach Una's handywork in time.

As gravity won the battle, they issued a collective groan of dismay. Landing right side up offered an encouraging moment, but when Ryker drew close, he saw the crust was cracked and blueberry filling spilled out one side.

Whiskey Jim stepped to Ryker's side and peered down at the sad scene. "There's no putting that back together."

"I reckon not."

"Maybe we should eat the parts still recognizable. If we don't the fox will be back to finish what he started."

Ryker caught a mischievous glint in the older man's eyes. Without further discussion, they sat down, one on either side of the destroyed pastry. Flicking off the leaves, they grabbed up the sturdier pieces of intact crust.

"That gal can sure bake a pie." Whiskey Jim grinned, blueberries staining his teeth.

Ryker laughed, enjoying a moment of camaraderie he hadn't felt in a long time. His line of work didn't encourage making friends. Before he could analyze or chase away the feeling as being detrimental to his peace of mind, MacTavish came loping around the corner. The dog approached tail wagging and mouth drooling. Evidently, he too enjoyed his mistress' baked goods.

Ryker sneaked a tidbit to the creature. If he couldn't win over the woman, he could at least win over the dog. As the hound came back to scarf down more, Ryker worried if too many berries might be harmful for the animal. He tried to dissuade MacTavish, but the big galoot was determined to fight for his share. As Ryker fended off the dog, Whiskey Jim laughed and gobbled up more of the salvageable morsels.

****

"What have you done to my pie!" More unladylike

words came to mind at the sight of her hard work gone to ruin.

For a moment, everybody, including the dog, seemed frozen in time as three pairs of guilt-ridden eyes stared up at her. Sitting in the dust, blueberry filling on their faces and hands, both men appeared about eight years old, not an easy feat for Mr. Jim. They began speaking simultaneously, offering no understandable excuse as their words were mixed with pie and made no sense to her.

"And even you, MacTavish. You mongrel traitor." The dog whined and grazed one paw across his muzzle trying to knock loose the piecrust crumbs. "You're in trouble too, mister." Hurrying to her side, the deerhound turned and growled at the men as if they were wholly responsible and he'd had nothing to do with the ruined pie.

"It was the fox." Ryker managed a coherent sentence as he gained his feet.

"A likely story."

"It's true. We were just passing by when a stealthy fox decided to steal your pie." Mr. Jim grabbed the windowsill and pulled himself upright, leaving a blueish handprint in the process.

Ryker stripped a handful of leaves off a nearby aspen tree and swiped them across his face and hands, removing most of the blueberry evidence.

Mr. Jim retrieved a red bandana from his pocket and cleaned up as well. "He upset the pie before we could stop him. Seemed a shame for such a work of art to go to waste."

At least the strawberry pie had survived, a consolation of sorts, she supposed. One pastry would have to be enough for tomorrow's gathering. She had no time or inclination to pick more blueberries.

Up on all fours, hackles raised, MacTavish set to barking as the culprit in question darted from behind the far side of the cabin and scrambled into the underbrush. "Stay, MacTavish. The damage is done and you got more pie than he did." With a pitiful whine the hound returned to her side.

Believing the destruction hadn't been the fault of the men, her temper cooled. And at the sight of Mr. Jim and Ryker she couldn't suppress a giggle. Being tired, her levity once underway was hard to contain, and soon all three were sharing a hardy laugh. Even MacTavish howled and rolled on the ground.

"I'm truly am sorry about your pie," Ryker said when they stopped to catch their breath. "And a delicious one it was."

With his captivating appeal turned on full force, he seemed younger and innocent of the reason for which he'd come barging into her world. She'd like to see that side of the man more often. But his philosophy regarding ancient treasures stood as solidly between them as a cavern wall, and her unsettled mood returned. "I'd best rescue the remaining pie before we lose a second one."

Mr. Jim carefully lifted the pastry from the windowsill and handed her the tin. As she turned to leave, Ryker called out. "Thank you for allowing me to stay here until I can make other arrangements."

So that's all she was to him, a convenience. And how quickly he'd gone from a one night stay to an open-ended invitation. She let his transgression ride. "Rather primitive conditions, but you're welcome."

"I can't think of any place I'd rather be."

At the sincerity behind his words, a thrill scampered through her. She cut the feeling short. Being an itinerant mercenary, Mr. Landry was practiced at insinuating his needs and desire onto whomever got in his way, and also quite good at giving people what he decided they wanted. What she wanted, deep inside, took her by surprise. Crushing the urge, she shifted her glance to the dead blueberry pie.

"Bury what's left or throw the scraps out in the woods for our naughty fox. I don't want an ant pile or some no good mangy critters lingering beneath my kitchen window." Irritated by the loss of the pie and the way Ryker toyed with her emotions, she didn't hide her displeasure.

"It's possible her last remark was directed toward the two of us." Mr. Jim's words gave her a moment of satisfaction.

****

What a shame he was always watching Una walk away with her head high and her back rigid, rather than seeing her running happily toward him. Ryker had envisioned the latter quite vividly. He wasn't accustomed to having his charming personality ignored. But all in good time.

"Let's do what we've been told and then make for camp," Whiskey suggested.

Using flat pieces of bark, the two of them scooped up the pie remnants and chucked the whole shebang into the bushes. Then without a word or backward glance, Whiskey Jim headed for the canyon. Collecting his horse, who had strayed during the commotion, Ryker followed.

Curious thing, he'd never seen Whiskey Jim with a horse, only on foot with his walking stick. Yet he'd seen the man in town. Surely the distance was more than an easy walk for him. Where did he keep his horse, and where did he disappear to in between his frequent visits to Una's property?

A curtain of mystery obscured this old man—their conversations rarely revealing anything of a personal nature. Ryker knew when someone was blowing smoke up his duster, and he was determined to find out more.

Chapter Twelve

The day of the eclipse broke crystal clear. Nary a cloud could be seen, not even atop Pike's Peak. And the Colorado sky shown so intensely blue, to admire the setting hurt one's eyes.

Una drank in the warmth. Anticipation seemed to hum in the air, the sound tangible as if she stood beside her beehives. Even the Earth knew today was special.

Wallace came over for a morning hug, The Countess remained a bit more reserved. She seemed happy here, although occasionally she stood staring off in the direction from which she came. Perhaps she had donkey-friends there and missed them.

Opening the holding pens, Una stood back as her tribe of goats bounded to freedom and their morning graze. Then she pumped water into the trough which the donkeys favored. They weren't fond of drinking from the creek.

Wallace and The Countess ambled along behind the goats, and with one arm draped over the gelding's neck, Una followed them into the pasture. "You two seem to be getting on famously." Wallace nosed her thigh as if in agreement, and she hugged his strong neck and scratched one ear.

Unlike horses and sheep, the goats and donkeys were browsers not grazers, and nothing was safe in their midst. She glanced at the sturdy fence around her garden. Only the ducks, goose, and chickens were allowed in there to eat the bugs and not the produce. Netting hung on tall poles protected the flock from overhead predators and MacTavish knew to watch for the fox.

With everybody happily munching away, her little corner of the world felt in-balance, and she nearly skipped back to the cabin stopping only once to collect an armload of split wood. Stacking the fuel beside the woodstove, she began shucking peas. She loved peas. Savory bright nuggets of springtime kept safe in the pod just waiting to be enjoyed in the heat of summer.

The cornbread she made yesterday had turned out perfect, and the ingredients were laid out for the honey cake to be baked in her cast iron frying pan. Cut up with dill, the potatoes and eggs set to boil would be a great addition to the celebration meal.

Jim insisted on bringing antelope steaks to fry in the outdoor firepit. When alone, she didn't favor the eating of meat, wouldn't dream of consuming the goats, ducks, or chickens she cared for like children. But she didn't begrudge others their preference and partook with gratitude of what was graciously offered.

"Hello in the cabin."

At the sound of Ryker's voice Una jumped, sending a handful of peas rolling across the table. Leaping up she grabbed the wayward vegetables and tossed them in with the rest, then turning to face the door, she smoothed out her skirt and worked at arranging her recalcitrant hair. Damp with perspiration from the heat of the woodstove and her morning labors, her locks curled and spiraled at will.

"Come in." Heart fluttering like a humming bird

caged in her chest, she could barely get the words out.

Ryker peeked in the open door, then stepped over the threshold. A jaunty bandana tied loosely around his neck indicated he'd taken extra care in dressing. His hair appeared wet and slicked back from a recent washing, and he carried a small tin pail which he held out to her.

"More blueberries." The sparkle of amusement in his eyes made her feel younger than she was, and prettier than she knew she appeared right now.

"Thank you." She accepted his thoughtful gesture and set the bucket on the dry sink. There weren't enough for another pie, but adding them to the honey cake would make a nice and sweet surprise.

Ryker grazed his hand across his shoulder and arm. "Whiskey tended to my injury already. He declared the wound was healing well, then before I could protest, he smeared more of your ointment on a clump of moss, slapped the lot in place, and wrapped her up. I hope he knows what he's doing."

"I'm sure we can trust in his knowledge of herbal cures. He's schooled in many things from times past."

"Knowledge and trust are two different things. Trust doesn't come easily."

"No. Not for any of us."

"Old Whiskey Jim is a puzzlement. And he's hiding something."

His statement took Una by surprise, and she faced him head on. He appeared dead serious. "This land is special. Many people from many places are drawn here for various reasons. I've learned not to pry. We all have secrets, Mr. Landry. I'm guessing even you."

****

He definitely had a few life experiences he'd never felt comfortable sharing with anyone. Since everyone had choices, much of what he'd been through was of his own making. But other times the machinations of men and the design of fate created inexplicable moments—you had to have been there to understand.

But those recollections were not meant for a day like today. "True enough," he agreed, putting the subject to rest. "I'm glad you have MacTavish to watch over you."

"Are ye worried for my safety, Mr. Landry?"

"What if I am? After the incident by the cave, you should be too."

"Then I say thank you. But be happy for me rather than concerned. I have much here for which to be thankful."

Irritated with himself for betraying his apprehensions for her wellbeing, he gave a non-committal, "If you say so."

Arms outstretched, and hands raised palm up, she stood as if welcoming some kind of life force. "Good intentions are often more powerful than the pistol you wear in keeping both the land and me safe."

More powerful...and interesting choice of words. And she spoke as if the land were a living being close to her heart. Una reminded him of the healing women of the West Indies. They were connected to the land and respected for their special gifts.

As she went back to shucking peas, he glanced around her cabin with a more discerning eye. The last time here he was in pain and didn't notice the bunches of herbs tied and hung to dry from the main crossbeam. A small wooden bucket beside her baskets of wool contained a collection of colorful rocks. And the upper shelf in the kitchen held several mason jars containing various concoctions, one resembling the medicine she'd given him to speed his wound recovery.

Catching him staring, she favored him with a smile, tiny crinkles at the corners of her green eyes adding to the merriment of her expression. With her burnished red hair and apparent love for the land and animals, Una seemed the perfect person to live in this secluded vale surrounded by a canyon brimming with tall tales and legends.

Inhaling the tantalizing aroma of food and dowsed in the fragrance of the hanging herbs and spices, he believed this woman was capable of casting a spell on him. She needn't bother, he was already smitten. Yes, smitten. Never in his life had that term seemed relevant. The rampage of feelings she stirred in him ran the gambit from wanting to bed her, to wanting to protect her, to wanting to walk away from her as fast as possible.

She was a danger to his way of life. Or maybe his way of life was a danger to his happiness. Una confused him. Made him unsettled. And what a fetching picture she created, one easy to commit to memory and long for at a later date. But he wasn't fond of wasting time on lonely reflections—he needed to vacate the cabin.

"Anything I can do for you other than get out of your way?"

"More firewood is always appreciated."

He hurried outside, relieved to have a legitimate reason for performing any activity other than standing and staring at her like a randy schoolboy. Returning with all the split wood he could carry, he deposited the armload by the stove and turned to leave.

"Thank you, Ryker."

For the first time, she'd called him by his Christian name, and dang, he liked the sound of it wrapped in her unpredictable Scottish burr.

"You're welcome, Una." His reply came over his shoulder as he left. The jaunty tune she hummed hesitated for a moment. He smiled. Did she like the sound of her name on his lips as well?

In the front yard, he studied the landscape to determine the best place for them to watch the eclipse. He had to admit, the event had captured his imagination. And the viewing would be even more special because he was sharing the experience with Una. Unfortunately, Whiskey Jim had also been invited. Gut instinct told Ryker the man wasn't being honest, and it seemed they would always be at odds about the artifacts. Yet despite the red flags, Ryker liked the old man.

As Ryker investigated an old wooden cart, a fun idea sprang to mind. One of the two shafts used for pulling no longer existed. Undaunted, he grabbed hold of the one remaining, and gritting his teeth, he tugged. Nothing. Time and the elements had embedded the big wooden wheels into the dirt. A quick search in the nearby shed offered a length of rope and a new plan.

Tying onto the one good strut, he played out the rope to where the always curious Wallace stood with his head hanging over the pasture fence. "Come on, boy, I need your help. It's for your mistress. For Una." At the sound of her name, the donkey's ears tipped forward, and he didn't fuss as Ryker attached the rope to his halter. "Backup, boy, just a little, you can do it.

Back, go on back."

With a toss of his head Wallace retreated a few steps. The rope went taut, but the wagon didn't move. "Pull harder, boy. You can do it." The donkey renewed his efforts. With a creak and a groan, the old transport tore loose lumbering forward on big wobbly wooden wheels. Out of the shade and into the sun near the garden, they reached the perfect spot for viewing. "Whoa now. Good lad. You did good." He unhooked the hemp from Wallace and neatly coiled the rope as he walked back to the wagon.

Gathering hay from the floor of the barn, he placed several armloads into the wagon. For a stepping-stone, he rolled a large rock closer. Admiring his handiwork, he noticed there was just enough room for two.

****

When the honey cake was done everything would be ready.

Mr. Jim had already arrived, and he and Ryker were frying the meat. But why was the old worn-out wagon by the garden? What had Ryker come up with now? He always seemed full of ideas—not all to her liking—although he hadn't mentioned the relics lately. She supposed the money he would receive for such a find was quite the temptation.

The coming of the eclipse had spawned ideas of making money too. Tents had been set up in the Garden of the Gods, where spectators could watch the eclipse for twenty-five-cents. Even churches were making a profit—leasing the windows in their steeples at an amazing fifty cents a person. Fortunately, they could watch today's display for free.

But best of all, Colorado would enjoy the national

spotlight again. This time for a scientific reason, proving the state had more to offer besides gold rush fever.

Back in Scotland, at Granny Riona's side, she'd learned about the movement of the stars, moon, and sun, and the magic of the world around her. She felt the spirit of the rocks and trees, hence her love of the cave and the canyon. She even felt a connection to the formidable white panther. Granny would have loved to have seen such a spectacle as the eclipse.

Returning to the stove, hands protected with a towel, she removed the honey cake baked in her cast iron frying pan. How, she wondered, would the celestial display affect all that dwelled here?

As she began transferring the food to the outdoor area, Ryker spotted her and hurried over to help. "There's a basket of utensils by the door if ye've a mind tae gimme a hand." She shouldn't enjoy having the contrary rogue around—but oh how she did. His soulful eyes and manly qualities inspired feelings that shot straight through her without logic or worry over consequences.

"That's the last of what I've prepared. I guess we're ready." She set the butter beside the cornbread and allowing herself a moment of pride she surveyed the array of food on the makeshift table.

"Perfect timing," Mr. Jim chimed in. He speared the roasted steaks, transferring them from the wire grid he'd placed over the fire to a wooden salver.

Una was hungry. She hadn't prepared such a feast in two years. The last time being Christmas '76. From then on, she stopped celebrating holidays or special days of any kind. At first, after losing Hamish, she went all out, reveling for the two of them, acting as if he were still with her enjoying the merriment. Then she faced reality and gave up the false cheer because in the long run pretending only made her feel worse.

Today she would be making a new memory, celebrating in earnest with the new people in her life. They had no expectations of her nor she of them. How liberating.

As the moon nipped away at the edge of the sun, they filled their plates with the side dishes and sat on the collection of logs she'd rolled and arranged under the cottonwood trees. Amber glasses in hand they alternately chewed and gazed upward.

"Good fixins, Mrs. MacLaren."

"Thank you, and your contribution is most welcome, Mr. Jim."

"Hey, I brought the blueberries," Ryker piped up as he shoved more honey cake in his mouth.

"Also a welcome addition."

Eating outside on this beautiful day with these two personable fellows took on the likes of a family picnic. She glanced around at the animals, her real family. Should she do anything special to prepare them for what was to come? Would even the bees be confused? She supposed letting nature take its course was the only answer.

Soon an eerie quiet hung in the air and a strange dimness hid in the shadows making her want to squint as if her eyesight had begun to fail.

Done eating, they stacked their plates and covered the remaining food. Ryker clasped her left hand in his and led her to the hay filled wagon. "Here, hop on up."

"And what is all this aboot?" Hands on her hips,

Una faced the old wagon full of hay.

"It's for you. Best viewing seat in the county."

Ryker beamed at his own genius. His consideration touched her deeply, which irritated her rather than making her happy. Why did he have to be so nice—and so handsome?

"Oh, it's quite a fine idea. But I'm maer worried aboot the animals than mah comfort." Made schoolgirlish and giddy by his nearness, her brogue thickened. "What will they be thinking o' this darkness in th' middle o' th' day? And ah canna be lollygagging around for hours. Eclipse or no eclipse, there's chores tae be done once it's over." Cross at falling prey to Ryker's charming ways and her befuddled emotions, her words came out tart and unappreciative. He scowled, making her regret her tone

"I'm sorry for my rude reply. This is a wonderful idea. I'm not accustomed to being looked after with such concern."

"Well, maybe you should be."

Her independent streak flared for a moment. If nothing else, becoming a widow had taught her to rely on herself. She didn't need a man taking care of her. But needing and wanting were two different things. She wanted to be cherished and pampered—at least on occasion. If only he were the man for the job.

"I'll keep your words in mind. Mr. Jim, what was the schedule ye read in last week's paper at the barber shop?"

"I wrote the information down so's there'd be no possibility of missing the display." The older man fished a crumpled paper from his back pocket, cleared his throat, and read. "The conjunction, already begun, started at two-sixteen, totality to occur at three-thirty and end at three-thirty-three. Shows over at four-thirty-one. They got it timed down to the minute."

Tucking the paper away, he consulted his pocket watch. "Looks like we're right on the money."

Using the stepping stone, and steadied by Ryker's grip on her elbow, she clambered aboard the cart. Her skirt hiked up indecently high exposing a good bit of ankle and calf, and judging by the quirky smile on Ryker's face, he hadn't missed the display. Scooting around and tucking her legs beneath her, she left room in the cart for him. This also did not escape Ryker's attention.

He pulled himself up, and lounged on the far side, keeping a gentleman's distance yet ending up close enough for her to feel his presence. She gripped her viewing glass so hard she nearly cut her hand.

"Your hair is even more appealing in this mysterious half-light."

What a bald-faced lie, and an obvious attempt at winning her favor. Her hair, a tangled mess from rushing around and cooking, couldn't appear much worse. She wasn't buying his overt compliment. "I'll wager I'll look even better when the light is completely gone."

He grinned and shook his head as if he knew he'd been caught bending the truth.

The goats had come back across the pasture to congregate near the gate. Ever vigilant, the two donkeys stood nearby tossing their heads and pacing about. They all seemed aware something was afoot.

Sitting in silence began to feel awkward, and because talking while gazing at the sun through the glass came easier than face to face, Una hazarded a question. "From where do you hail, Ryker Landry?"

"I guess it depends where I am as to where I'm from. In Colorado I'm from back East. Back East I was newly returned from Spain. In Spain, Brazil had been my previous port of call."

"My goodness. You're a citizen of the world."

"Yes, I suppose so."

"And where will you be heading in order to say you are from here?"

"I haven't decided."

A none answer which left room for possibilities. "Have you ever been to Scotland?"

"Yes, and the Hebrides, a wild and beautiful place."

"I miss my homeland, but my family is gone."

"I've no family to miss either. Being orphaned isn't easy."

Ryker's words seemed from the heart. No wonder he was a wanderer. As their inner most feelings met and entwined, they sighed in unison and gazed up at the sky.

What power in the universe designed the paths we walked? And who decided which paths crossed and which paths never met or suddenly ended? She figured God was probably busy with important matters with little time to worry about how our lives unfolded once he sent us on our way. Fate was the culprit, laughing at our best laid plans. At least God sent us angels and spirit guides to help us with the journey

A second piece of honey cake in one hand, Mr. Jim rolled a stump closer with his other, and took a seat beside the wagon. "The best part is starting," he announced, his excitement managing to make it out around his mouth full of cake.

This was it, Una's heart beat faster. The donkeys huffed and whined and the goats pressed closer. With one eye turned upward, the chickens, ducks, and goose hurried awkwardly toward their nighttime roosting quarters. Little by little the sun disappeared. Shadows turned to mist, and as the light slipped away, a softness layered their surroundings. When the last ray of sun winked out, darkness fell—complete and startling. Stars shone in the sky, the air grew noticeably cooler, as an eerie stillness settled over them.

Unsteady at the sudden shift, she reached out with her free hand and found Ryker's waiting. Fingers interlaced they held fast as the sun was totally obliterated and a blaze of gold ringed the eye of darkness.

"It's magical," she exhaled the words in awe.

"Glad I lived to see such a sight," Mr. Jim agreed, wonderment coloring his words too.

Ryker remained silent, but his grip tightened ever so slightly indicating the display was not lost on him either. One hundred and ninety-one seconds later, the first ray of sunlight escaped the blackness and speared down to Earth reversing the phenomenon,

The rooster crowed as if morning had come again in the afternoon. The donkeys joined in with hardy hee-haws. In a discord of maahs and baahs, and as if late for an important appointment, the goats rushed back out to pasture.

Following months of anticipation, the culmination of the event left Una woozy, and she flopped back onto the hay, continuing to stare through her glass as the fire ball grew larger and larger.

"Praise the Saints, what a grandiose sight."

Elbow bent, his head propped up in his hand, Ryker stretched out at her side, the length of his body mere inches from hers. He no longer seemed fascinated with the moon and sun. She shifted her viewing glass and met his gaze. He wanted to kiss her. The wonton idea appealed to her as well—quite deeply.

They drew closer, their lips separated by the width of a butterfly wing. Then the creak and groan of splintering wood filled the air. The left wheel fell off and the tumbril tipped sharply sideways. Ryker gathered her close, and with a flurry of hay and matching yelps of surprise, they toppled to the ground.

Careening to a halt, wrapped in one another's arms, Una couldn't stop laughing. Rolling onto her back she pressed her hands to her stomach, but the belly laughs kept coming. Giving up, she rejoiced in the moment, not remembering the last time such gaiety had seized control of her body and robbed her of her good senses.

Upsetting the stump, Mr. Jim clattered to his feet. Hands on his thighs, he bent forward and peered down at them. "You two all right?" Still chuckling, they both nodded, and he laughed too. "Nothing like dinner and a show."

Mr. Jim's mirth stopped as he straightened and glanced toward the trail leading from the main road to her property. "Company's coming."

Una went on the alert. Mr. Jim held out a hand to help her up, and she grabbed the offered assistance and scrambled upright. Ryker gave her backside a gentle boost. Then he was at her side, one hand at the small of her back, the other on the revolver at his hip.

Chapter Thirteen

Whoever approached did so at a fast clip. Trail dust twisted and swirled into the air behind the speeding carriage.

"Oh dear, that's Kate and Jordie." Una wrung her hands. "There must be trouble. Kate is with child and near due. Thay wouldna drive so fast unless there was an emergency."

As the team of horses careened to a stop, Una ran to Kate's side of the still rocking carriage. To her surprise she saw her friend held a wee bairn in her arms.

"Kate, what's happened, what's wrong?"

"He came early. Two days ago. Oh, Una he isn't well, and Doc went to Denver to see the eclipse with his sister. The baby is slow to thrive. My milk is thrifty, and he has a fever."

Una assisted Kate down from the carriage, and with an arm across her friend's shoulder, she ushered her toward the cabin. "Come inside. We'll see what ails him. He's got a beautiful head of hair. Not red, but you can't have everything." This brought a weak smile from Kate, and her panic seemed to recede a bit.

Grabbing a woolen blanket, Una bunched the mohair bundle on the table, and they cozied the infant within the folds. His wee thready pulse beat too fast to count, and the poor little mite didn't fuss or cry, even when she moved his arms and legs to check for injury. "Sit, Kate, before you fall over. I can see by the dark smudges beneath your eyes, you've had no sleep. And probably not enough food."

"Yes, but the baby. That's all that matters."

"You matter too." She hugged her friend fiercely, showering her with light and love. "Once the fever is down, the bairn will need you more than any medicine. Are you healing properly?"

"Yes. I'm just tired, there was much blood."

"But it's stopped?"

"Much less now. Only a scant amount."

Una stepped to the cabin door. "Ryker, make a plate o' food for Jordie and bring one for Kate. Mr. Jim, I'm needing cold water from the well. Swiftly, please, and thank you both."

While her instructions were carried out, Una collected several Mason jars from the shelves in the kitchen. Coneflower and oregano for the babe's fever and stuffy nose. Shephard's Purse and Chickweed to purify and fortify Kate's blood, and mint to sooth the little one's stomach.

Using mortar and pestle she ground away. After the water arrived and a plate was set before Kate, Una sprinkled the herbs on top of the tatties and stirred them in well. "Sorry, the consistency on the potatoes will be a bit crunchy. I'll give you more herbs to take home with instructions on how to brew a tea. The leaves are much easier to stomach when distilled."

Kate didn't seem to mind the extra ingredients as she ate with gusto.

"What's his name?" Una asked as she ground different herbs for the infant and soaked them to make a treacle.

"Jedidiah"

"Aye, a good strong name. I've a feeling he'll be livin' up to it."

"I pray so, Una. Thank you for the comfort and food. I was hungrier than I knew."

"Since ye'v cleaned your plate like a good lassie, I need you to sponge the wee babe off with this cool water. But keep the wool around him, we want to bring down his fever but not give him a chill. I'm going to fetch goat milk from my nanny who delivered late and is still nursing."

Grabbing a small metal container, she left the cabin and headed for the barn. Three worried faces turned as they followed her progress. "I'm hopeful all will be well, Jordie. He's a braw lookin' laddie," she reassured the new father.

Jordie beamed with pride. "We're so thankful for your help."

Without a fuss, Blossom, the goat, gave up a full pail of milk. Back at the cabin, Una dipped the twisted corner of a clean towel into the still warm liquid. The baby began to suck immediately and with enthusiasm.

As Kate kept up the process of dipping and feeding, Una strained the soaking herbs out of the water, then she boiled down the liquid to make a concentrate which she added to the milk.

Jordie stuck his head in the door. "I had to know how he was doing." Kate's happy face answered his question. Stepping forward he crouched at his wife's side, a joyful expression replacing his furrowed brow of concern.

"I'll pack up everything you need to continue with

this at home." Una stuffed little bags of herbs in a small wooden box. "You must not neglect taking your curatives too, Kate."

"I'll make sure she does," Jordie promised.

Kate set aside the feeding cloth for just a moment to give her husband a kiss. Kicking his legs, the babe let out a wailing cry. Both parents appeared startled then chuckled with relief.

"That's the first time he's cried hale and hardy rather than whimpering. He definitely is feeling better." Kate returned to the dipping and feeding, and murmurs of satisfaction accompanied the babe's suckling sounds. Una watched the three of them. She was happy for her friends. Kate would be a wonderful mother, just as she was a wonderful wife and teacher.

At one time, Una had aspirations of motherhood.

Ryker's voice carried in from the yard as he conversed with Mr. Jim. Not with this rascal, of course. But recently she'd imagined new beginnings not limited by what she had experienced in the past. For a while, she'd lost the spirit of wonder to see what the next day might bring—until now.

****

Ryker watched Una take control of the dire situation. So slight in form, her strength continued to surprise him.

"She's a bit of a miracle, isn't she?" Whiskey Jim stared at the cabin.

Apparently, most people who knew Una had a place in their heart for her. He could see why. If he were serious about stealing her affections, the whole world would be his competition. But, of course, he wasn't serious. Not for a moment. He was only having a bit of fun.

Turning away he leaned against the lopsided hay cart. When they'd been thrown into one another's arms, Una's laughter had been music to his ears. Deep and hardy, she hadn't held back in her enthusiasm, and the glimpse of trim ankle and calf had enticed the lusty side of his nature. What would she be like sharing other moments of even greater excitement?

He kicked at the broken wheel lying on the ground. He was spending too much time daydreaming about her. Days had passed since he'd thought seriously about the artifact he'd come to find. And if he failed to deliver, Mr. Cockrell's ire would know no bounds. Yet Ryker didn't want Dax Thompson to have the prize either.

Kate and the baby emerged from the cabin, and Una followed carrying a small wooden box, another parcel tucked under her arm. The happiness in Kate's eyes indicated an upturn in the infant's condition.

As the others gathered around, talking and laughing like the old friends they were. Ryker remained at a distance, an outsider. Fading into the trees, he slipped away toward the canyon and cave, a passel of worries needling the mind of the free spirit he claimed to be.

Reaching the campsite he'd been sharing with Whiskey Jim, Ryker packed up his belongings. With the eclipse over, the ruckus in town would fade and there would be room for let at the hotel. Nothing would beat his currant accommodations as far as being close to Una and the cave, but he'd decided to change his strategy.

If he didn't relocate for a little while, he feared

Whiskey Jim would never vacate the area. And in the end, putting all these illusions of a different life aside, he knew he had to get his hands on what he'd come here for.

****

Curly tried not to fidget as Mr. Pritchard read him the riot act.

"As soon as the tourists have thinned out and are no longer gallivanting all over creation, you boys get back to making sure, one way or another, that woman is gone."

"Yes sir, Mr. Pritchard. We were dead sure poisoning the water would work. Hadn't been no rain for weeks when we doused the stream. Then a raging thunderstorm came up out of a clear blue sky diluting and washing downstream all the arsenic we dumped in the water. The fence cutting went afoul too."

"I already know what didn't work, and I don't want excuses, Curly. I want results."

"Yes sir, boss. We're on it."

Curly left the *big house* and stood in the yard. Frustration boiled in his belly, and he swiped off his hat and slapped the canvas against his thigh—dust billowed out from the impact.

Dang woman. The widow MacLaren was nothing but trouble. He didn't see why they couldn't take care of her like they had her husband. But Mr. Pritchard said after getting away with the *fatal accident*, and their other deadly escapade, they shouldn't press their luck.

Maybe the Boss was right. This lady had friends in town so she would be missed, and her death likely to raise a rumpus. Since that chance thunderstorm, the land had dried out. Maybe a fire would do the trick.

They could give it a try come morning.

Chapter Fourteen

Una stood beside Strawberry Creek and offered up her morning prayers, asking especially for kindness to dwell in her heart for all creatures.

The pesky fox who tried to steal her pie was back and turning his attention to her fowl and eggs. In this instance, her *live and let live* philosophy was hard to honor and testing her patience. Today, she'd left MacTavish to roam near the garden and coops.

Standing beside the running water, she felt restless, but the land felt peaceful and yesterday seemed like a dream. Following the excitement of the eclipse and the unexpected arrival and departure of Kate, Jordie, and the baby, Ryker had disappeared and Mr. Jim had left too. She could almost feel the loneliness in the breeze.

How quickly she'd grown accustomed to the sound of voices and the enjoyment of interaction with beings other than her animals. T'would have been easier if she'd never met any of them—but less enriching in heart and soul.

A sound caught her attention as a deer came to drink at the stream. For a while, like the goats, the woodland creatures had stopped coming to the stream as if the water were tainted. After the rainstorm she bid wash the land clean, they returned. The need to call down the storm had come to her with a fierceness not to be denied. And whatever had been wrong no longer seemed a threat. A good thing too, as their alternative water source, the Arkansas River, had receded, turning sluggish, the banks deep with mud.

Spotting the goats and donkeys on the hill near the bee hives, she grabbed a downed branch for a walking stick and ambled up the incline to join them. When last she checked, the honey was only fifty percent capped. If she were patient there would be even more ready to harvest, and each jar she sold was money in the bank.

At her approach Wallace and The Countess huffed out a greeting. The goats glanced up, and recognizing her, quickly returned to grazing. Warm from climbing the hill, she sat down in the shadow cast by the stacks of wooden boxes.

Wallace drew near, and lowering his head within easy reach, he begged for a good ear rubbing. Such a kind funny face, how could she resist?The Countess remained hesitant. Una hoped somehow they would come to trust one another.

Wallace's head jerked up, knocking into her shoulder, and she heard voices coming closer—men's voices.

Peering around the edge of the box, she chastised herself for not bringing the rifle. With Ryker and Mr. Jim about more often, she'd gotten out of the habit of toting the heaving firearm from place to place. Another mistake created by depending on others.

"This ought to be far enough, boys. The wind is behind us and should sweep the flames down the hill toward the cabin."

Flames!

Wallace and The Countess brayed in the most abrasive of terms. The goats ran in all directions. Una grabbed a rock, gained her feet, and chucked the stone at the nearest cowboy. "Get off my property you wretched blackguards."

The rock struck the man's thigh, causing more surprise than pain. All three men began to laugh. The one she'd struck held a lit torch.

"We don't want your kind around here, lady. You should have taken the hint." He urged his horse even closer, and bending sideways he tried to ignite a small tuft of tall dry grass.

Una ran forward and grabbed his arm. He kicked her to the ground. Wallace went wild, charging the man and his horse. The Countess knocked over the nearest bee hive. Angry at being disturbed, the bees shot up into the air. Then turning in unison, they sought the unfamiliar intruders, swarming the men on horseback.

Screams of pain rang out from the three caballeros and their horses. The animals lunged about in confusion, charging first one direction then the next. The leader of the group dropped the torch. Trying to save the parched ground, Una crawled toward the impending fire, and dragging the shawl from her shoulders she smothered the smoldering grass. Then she rolled the discarded torch in the dirt to extinguish the glowing end.

MacTavish must have noticed the altercation. The dog's baying and howling filled the air as he headed her way.

"Let's get out of here." The man could barely get the words out between yelps of pain as the bees continued their stinging assault. With no concern for her safety underfoot, he wheeled his mount around and one of the horse's hooves struck a glancing blow to

Una's head, landing her flat on her back.

The last thing she remembered was the sound of horses galloping away and the feel of the hard earth beneath her body.

****

Sitting in the hotel eatery, Ryker nursed his second cup of morning coffee. After the eclipse, the town had cleared out in record time as if gold had been discovered farther up the road. Even the saloon into which he could see from his chair was quiet and nearly empty.

Then three cowpokes stumbled in and attached themselves to the bar, and a ruckus commenced disturbing the silence. The men were the same ones who had harassed Mrs. MacLaren in the general store. Their attitudes were even more obnoxious today. One pounded on the top of the bar as he growled out his demand. "We're gonna need the whole bottle."

"What in tarnation happened to you three?" The barkeep set up shot glasses, uncorked the whiskey, and set all within reach.

"Damn goat woman set a swarm of bees on us."

Goat woman. Ryker's sat up straighter, and his stomach clenched.

"Appears you men got the worst of it." The man behind the bar dared to chuckle at the three miserable cowboys.

"This time." The hatred accompanying the words had the barkeep taking a step back, and he found work to do elsewhere.

Ryker tossed the necessary money on the table and made his way out the door.

****

Una's eyes fluttered open, and she shrank back at the flood of pain and sunlight.

MacTavish sat at her side, and Wallace and The Countess peered down at her as she lay in the dirt.

Her head throbbed unmercifully, and when she ran her hand over her right temple, she felt a large lump and her hand came back sticky with blood. What had happened? She couldn't reason clearly.

MacTavish whined and licked her face. "Easy, laddie." She tried to push him away, but her arm felt weak and near useless. Wallace gently nudged her shoulder with his nose.

She began to shake, cold even as sunlight poured down from above. Where was her shawl? Using one hand she blindly felt the ground around her. Catching the wool by one corner, she dragged the covering closer and over her body. Part of the woven fabric was crunchy and smelled like charred wool. Fire—there had been fire. The cattlemen had been here with torches.

She sniffed the air, relieved she didn't smell smoke or hear the crackle of flames. There was nothing but quiet, no sounds of the men, just the breeze in the nearby trees and the buzzing of bees. Her bees… Oh no, had all her hives and honey been destroyed?

Easing up on one elbow, she squinted sideways trying to focus through the pain that sent her world spinning like the top whorl on her drop spindle. One stack of hives lay forlornly on its side, the wooden box broken, honey leaking out onto the ground. But the other two structures were still upright. At least all was not lost.

Shifting around, she forced herself onto her hands and knees. Nausea struck, and she vomited, the jarring action sending her vision once again into a tailspin. She must get to the cabin. Although she shivered uncontrollably, the day was growing hotter by the minute and she was feeling worse and worse.

Grabbing one of Wallace's front legs, she pulled herself hand over hand upward to her feet. Could she ride him? He stood at the ready like the gallant beast he was, but he was unbroken, and had never been ridden. To attempt mounting him might be asking for trouble.

Using Wallace for support, she shuffled along over to The Countess. Mr. Jim had mentioned she was broken and ridable if she so chose. With one arm over the jenny's neck for support, she urged her big girl over to a piece of broken hive box. The bees still sounded angry, but they seemed to recognize her and the donkey, and rather than launching an attack, they flitted around without direction as if wondering what had happened to their home laying smashed on the ground.

Grabbing a handful of short mane, and using the wood as a mounting block, Una gritted her teeth and crawled up onto the donkey's back. "Whoa, pretty lady. It's all right. I'm in need of your help."

Fatigued by the small exertion Una lay flat, arms and legs draped and dangling over The Countess' back and withers. Head throbbing and stomach churning, she clucked the donkey into action. "Go to the barn, girl. Go to the barn."

The Countess was more familiar with heading to the barn than the cabin. If they could make that distance, she could crawl the rest of the way.

As the jenny picked her way off the ridge, Una closed her eyes. Thank goodness the fire had been averted. But what was she going to do about these murderous cattlemen? She had just as much right here as did they. She hoped the ruffians suffered greatly from the bee stings.

Squinting her eyes open, she groaned in dismay. The Countess was going in the wrong direction. "No, ya daft creature, turn around." Plead as she may the stalwart donkey kept plodding along into the woods. Tears wet Una's cheeks. Glancing back, she saw MacTavish and Wallace following in their wake, leaving no one to watch the farm.

"Stay. Guard." She ordered the pair in the most authoritative voice her pain would allow.

Whining, the deerhound paced back and forth, but he held his position. Wallace stopped too—shaking and bobbing his head as if he were confused as to what to do.

Should she slide to the ground and try reaching the cabin on her own? Easing upright, she grew dizzier than before, and faint of heart. With a groan she lay flat again. Fearing to fall, she hugged the donkey, and welcomed the darkness.

****

After a quick search of Una's farm, Ryker's heart sank. The entrancing woman who strayed frequently into his thoughts seemed to have strayed completely out of sight and gone missing.

MacTavish guarded the cabin, which was empty. And only the gelding mingled with the goats. Cantering up the hill to the beehives, he saw the destruction and the scorched earth. These had to be the bees who had ravaged the cattlemen.

Starting from the hives, Ryker circled the property, calling Una's name as he went. Each time he came around he went farther out increasing the perimeter as he searched for her or signs of what happened. He also kept an eye out for the other donkey. Maybe the jenny had strayed during the commotion. Or maybe Una had ridden off on her—but why and to where?

For once he wished Whiskey Jim was around, he could have prevented the attack or helped in finding Una. She might even be with the older man. There were so many possibilities. None to his liking.

"Which way did she go, MacTavish."

The dog ran toward the woods, then returned as if not willing to leave his post. "We need to find her, boy." MacTavish sat down, not willing to budge. In this instance, Una had trained the dog too well. He supposed, considering what must've happened, having the dog guard the farm wouldn't hurt.

Ryker kept circling, searching for a sign. Being smaller than a horse and unshod, the donkey could pass leaving less of a trail. His next revolution brought him near the entrance to the cave and canyon. Here was the ideal opportunity to retrieve the artifact. Unobserved and uninterrupted, he could make as much noise as necessary to open up the back room.

He shook his head and kept going. There was a time he would have gone for the money rather than the woman.

****

"We got company." Harlen faded into the thicket and latched the hammer back on his rifle.

Another man on guard duty stood fast at his side. "Don't sound like more than one man. And he's making no attempt at being quiet."

"Maybe Whiskey Jim's a comin' for another visit.

136

Or do you suppose it's them Revenuers? I thought they was concentratin' their efforts up Denver way."

"Hard tellin' what those sneaky varmints might have in mind. Hush now, here they come"

At the snapping of underbrush and the sound of hooves nicking fallen timber, both men held their breath

"Well, I'll be a monkey's uncle." Harlen eased the hammer down on the rifle and stepped out into the clearing. "That's our Rosie, the donkey we sold to Whiskey Jim. Whoa, girl. Who you got there on your back?"

****

The voices cut through the blackness, and Una fought to open her eyes.

The dim forested atmosphere blurred, and she locked gazes with two men who stood staring at her. Had the brutal cattlemen returned? Mustering all her strength, she struggled to sit upright. They would show her no mercy—she must show no fear. As this noble intention surged through her weakened body, she tumbled sideways.

The two men rushed forward, cushioning her descent to the ground. Their voices seemed to come from far away.

"Sure enough, she's the woman owns those goats up north a piece. What she doin' here and what we gonna do with her, Harlan"

"Her head's a bleedin'. I reckon she took a knock to the old brainpan."

"Whiskey asked us to watch out for her. It'll be dark soon, so we better get her back to camp."

In her state of confusion, their words came too fast,

flittering through her mind like the tiny silver fishes in Strawberry Creek. She couldn't respond, she couldn't think.

The men lifted her up and between them they carried her farther into the woods. She struggled in their grasp, but they held fast, not viciously or hurtfully, but strong enough she couldn't break free. Her heated protests were a jumble even to her own ears.

"Don't be afeared, missy. We won't hurt ya."

The Countess followed at their side. Had the donkey betrayed or helped her? The pain pounding in her head made the choice an impossible one, and not truly caring she closed her eyes.

****

Ryker made camp for the night. He'd searched until darkness prevented further exploration. No use going around in circles. With MacTavish and Wallace defending the territory, the animals at the farm should be safe and all of them had access to grazing and water. Walking his mount to a pitiful pool of water, he let the gelding drink then staked him in a grassy area with a big tree for shelter.

The forested lowland to the south of Una's farm was thick with bracken and cottonwoods with boughs interlaced making passage difficult. In a marshy area, he'd collected cattail plants, and cutting up the roots he fried them for his supper.

Racked with worry, he sat beside the firepit and leaned against the saddle and blanket. Being a warm night, there was no use keeping up a roaring blaze, and as the coals cooled, smoke drifted lazily upward.

Ryker watched the gray tendrils dance and twist and disappear into a black sky studded with stars. Only one day ago he sat beside Una watching the daytime celestial display of the century. Now she was gone. Where could she be?

The cowpokes in the bar didn't sound as if they'd permanently resolved their issues with her, so he figured she was still alive. He didn't want to entertain any other possibilities. He felt a connection to Una, wanted to see her succeed at this difficult life she'd carved out for herself. Her steadfastness and outpouring of love for the animals and land made his own life seem a bit hollow and detached.

Lying on the hard ground, every previously torn muscle, broken bone, knife cut, and bullet hole screamed out at him tonight. Previously, he'd considered the scars proof of his character and endurance. Badges of courage proving he could conquer the wild dangers he chose to face. Now they seemed like markers of time, with little to show for the pain but distant memories of a younger man's folly. When the memories faded, he'd be left with nothing of permanence on this Earth.

The endless sky loomed overhead, making Ryker feel small. And with no one to talk to except his horse, he felt lonely.

The wind rustled the leaves and the howl of a coyote snapped him out of his revery. Maybe another log on the fire wouldn't hurt. He tossed on two for good measure and thought about the legends Whiskey Jim had recanted as they sat before a different fire.

Could the breast plate and flute really cause never healing burns, blindness, and madness? While other bounty for which he'd searched had come with warnings, none came with this feeling of doom. Was he willing to take the risk? These last few days, not dwelling on the artifact seemed to lift a weight off his shoulders.

And then there was Una. Her connection to unseen elements seemed ingrained in her and not a quality she'd recently acquired. Enchantment hovered near her. He gave a sarcastic snort of amusement. Whiskey Jim may have worked a bit of his own magic, transforming Ryker from a carefree mercenary into a protector of the land with a newfound set of ethics.

Bah, he was just tired. He'd always been a loner, the way he should remain.

Chapter Fifteen

Una lay motionless. Sunlight seeped through her closed eyelids alerting her the night had run its course and morning had arrived.

She remembered being awakened at intervals, the interruption making her angry by taking her from the blessed sleep where she could hide from the pain. She'd been too confused and weak to discover who kept bothering her or how she could make them stop.

At least the pain in her head had eased from excruciating to bearable. She moved her legs and was surprised when the entire bed shifted sideways. Gripping the mattress, she felt boards and rope. Squinting her eyes open, leaves and branches and the nose of The Countess wavered into view. The donkey's head was level with whatever Una lay upon.

"She's awake."

The words startled her, and the sudden appearance of men did not ease her apprehension.

"Who are you? Where am I?"

"My name's Harlan, ma'am. Rosie here brought you to us."

"Rosie?"

"The donkey Whiskey Jim bought from us and give to you."

"Oh, you mean The Countess."

The man chuckled and rubbed the donkey's

muzzle. "You come up in the world, old girl."

Una tried to sit up, setting the bed in motion again.

"Hold on, missy, or you'll upset this contraption. We didn't have a clean bed to put you in and didn't want you sleeping on the ground, so we rigged up an old door in the trees to lay you on. Sorry it's a bit uncomfortable. Hay covered with a tanned deer hide was all we had for a mattress."

No wonder her bones ached nearly as much as her head. But she was thankful they had taken care of her. She'd been more ill than she'd imagined. If The Countess had taken her to the cabin, she may have died. "On the contrary, it's wonderful, and quite ingenious."

The man glanced down and shuffled his feet as if embarrassed by her compliment.

"Let me give you a hand. See if you can stand." One man who appeared to be the leader of the clan, stepped forward as the others steadied the board.

Una remembered his voice. He was the one who awakened her in the night. She eased her legs over the side, reached for his arms, and slid to the ground.

Wobbly but upright, she glanced around. "You came to me in the night."

"Yes, ma'am. Name's Cletus. I was told if a person with a head injury sleeps too long and deep, they may never come back to the here and now."

"Yes, of course. Thank you. I'm in your debt." She glanced around. "Now I'm in need of a visit to the trees, if you ken my meaning."

"Here, take Rosie, I mean The Countess, to hang on to. You still be lookin' a might pale." He handed her the lead to the halter they'd placed on the donkey.

The braiding and knotwork were intricate and must

have taken hours and hours of painstaking effort to achieve. "My, what lovely workmanship."

"That would be Wiley's handiwork."

The man indicated doffed his hat and nodded, his face reddened by the attention he received.

"Folks would pay a handsome token for your labors."

Wiley appeared stunned by the idea and took a step back. "Just do it for my own entertainment, ma'am. Don't want to be mingling with no outsiders."

She'd heard rather terrifying stories about the group of ruffians living to the south of her, yet so far, these men had been courteous and kind. Whatever their reason for living in the woods, their privacy seemed important to them, and she had no intentions of prying or making them uncomfortable. "I understand."

She urged The Countess into motion and together they set off for the far thicket of brush and trees.

Finished with her necessary business, Una sat a moment on a fallen log to gather her wits and sort out her confusion. Hopefully all was well at the farm, but she mustn't tarry. The cattlemen might return to finish what they started, and regardless of how poorly she felt, defending her property came first—and she sorely missed MacTavish.

Stirred by these considerations, she gained her feet and made her way to the campfire where the men were preparing breakfast.

Hunger tugged at her stomach rather than nausea. A good sign she was on the mend. Although if she moved fast or bent low, pain throbbed in her brain,

"Sit here, ma'am." Cletus brushed the leaves and dust off of a stump for her.

****

Ryker eased around the corner of the shack, his rifle trained on the man standing beside Una. "Step away from the woman."

At the sound of his voice, all the men jumped and turned to face him. None wore a side arm. The one who carried an old Winchester rifle twitched as if debating on trying his luck.

"Don't do it." Ryker warned. "I'm not here to cause trouble. Just let the lady go, and we'll be on our way peaceably." This morning, he'd found a few strands of Una's shawl caught on a branch, and knowing a general direction, he'd made better progress

Una struggled to her feet. "Ryker. Don't shoot. They're friends. They took care of me when I was injured and confused." Stepping away from the men, she appeared unharmed and sounded sincere. But the men facing him were a grizzly lot and he wasn't about to trust them so easily.

"Calm down, mister. We meant the lady no harm. Whiskey Jim is a mutual friend, and we were just taking care of her the best we know'd how. She showed up here yesterday mighty sick and barely hanging onto the donkey what used to live here. Guess the critter couldn't figure where else to take her."

"Is he telling the truth?" Ryker need to be sure that's how she ended up here.

"Yes. This is Cletus, and he and all the lads have taken extremely good care of me."

Ryker lowered his rifle but shifted his free hand to the butt of his revolver.

"And whether or not she goes with you, mister, is up to her." Cletus' voice had a hard edge and the

144

squint-eyed glare accompanying the words alerted Ryker the man aimed to back up his words with action if need be.

"Thank you for your concern, Cletus." Una reassured the leader of the group. "I am acquainted with this man, as is Mr. Jim," Worry puckered her brow as she returned her gaze to Ryker. "Is everything all right at the farm? Those horrid cattlemen tried to burn me out. "

"Except for the smashed beehive, the property appeared okay. I closed up the cabin. MacTavish and Wallace refused to leave their posts and seemed to have things under control."

"Blessed be."

"I was mad with worry, Una. I saw blood by the hives."

At his words, she seemed taken aback as if his caring so much for her came as a surprise. Since seeing those signs of blood, his guts had been in a knot, with images too gruesome to recall. He was grateful she hardly seemed any worse for wear.

Cletus broke the lingering silence. "We were about to have breakfast." One man added more wood to the campfire, while the rest went about gathering the needed supplies. "You're welcome to join us, stranger."

"Name's Ryker Landry. Thank you for the invite and for looking after Mrs. MacLaren."

Fried backstrap, Johnnycakes, and good strong coffee made up their meal, and the talk was minimal, dominated by the sounds of eating and frogs croaking in the nearby marsh. A pile of firewood indicated the men spent time here year-round and were well entrenched. And the collection of funnels, jugs, and ballast bottles hinted at a possible occupation they were most likely reluctant to discuss.

"Not many men would be able to take us by surprise," Cletus pointed out.

"I've had lots of practice." Ryker left his explanation vague, yet meaningful.

Many a time his life had depended on stealth and cunning, but he hadn't expected to need such skills on his undertaking for Mr. Cockrell. This expedition was turning out to be complicated and troublesome, and certainly not worth what he was being paid. Then he glanced sideways at Una and a rush of desire hit him like an unanticipated punch to the gut. Perhaps the relic was no longer what he wanted. Maybe the prize worth going after was wrapped in glorious strands of red hair and came at the price of his heart and freedom.

The burliest of the men removed the kettle from the coals and filled a wooden tub with the hot water. Then he went around collecting the tin plates upon which they'd eaten. Taking the hint breakfast was over, Ryker gained his feet and helped Una to hers.

"Thank you again, gentlemen. I'd best get Mrs. MacLaren home."

Cletus stood, and the two men sized up one another. Drawn together by their mutual desire to protect the woman who stood between them, they would part as friends rather than enemies—this time. But Ryker wasn't naïve enough to think they wouldn't protect their own interests first if necessary. He could respect their resolve.

"Your lovely presence brightened our little corner of the world, ma'am. Sorry the circumstances were so desperate." Cletus doffed his hat, and the other men nodded goodbye.

"Your kindness won't be forgotten," Una promised. One man led the donkey to her and handed over the lead rope. "And I shall return the halter as soon as possible."

"No need," Wiley piped up. "Yours to keep as a memento of your visit."

"A treasured gift then."

Una at his side, Ryker led the donkey into the woods to where he'd tethered his horse. Tying the donkey to a branch, he gave Una a leg up. "Quite the conquest. You seem to have won the hearts of the whole lot of them."

"Are you a wee bit jealous then, Mr. Landry?" She added a slight smile as she settled into place, and he handed her the lead to the halter.

"Absolutely not. Just an observation." He swung up into the saddle and clucked his horse into a walk. "You are a troublesome female, and the last thing I need is trouble."

"And yet you seem to find disruption so readily."

****

They ambled along at a donkey's pace, uninterrupted until the flight of a large bird caught Ryker's attention. The turkey vulture, circling high above, dropped lower with each revolution. Una followed his gaze and gave a shiver. "Those birds never portent anything good."

He had to agree, and now there were two of the carcass-eaters.

"Maybe we should see what they've found."

Reluctantly he turned off to the left. The largest of the birds landed in the cottonwoods. The other one issued a low guttural hiss and dropped through the branches out of sight. Skirting around the patch of trees, they reached a small clearing and found the reason for the presences of the scavengers. A dead man lay on his back in the tall grass.

Ryker kicked his horse into a gallop scaring off the buzzard tearing at the body. Flapping its great wings and stirring up the dust, the vulture hopped to one side before reluctantly joining the other in the tree. Now two sets of beady black eyes, surrounded by blood red markings, glared down from above—waiting, ever waiting, for a chance to continue their meal.

The donkey snorted and gave a disgruntled halfhearted bray. Turning he saw Una unsuccessfully urging The Countess closer. The animal wanted no part of the death-smell wafting the air. Not happy with the situation either, Ryker's mount danced to one side.

Dismounting, he led his horse over to Una and handed off the reins. "Until we know what happened, I suggest you stay put."

Ignoring his own advice, Ryker drew closer, shocked to discover the body was that of Dax Thompson. His nemesis was fully clothed, his revolver still holstered. His hat, having tumbled from his head, rested off to one side. With his skin ashen, and his mouth contorted in a silent scream, he hadn't died peacefully. His eyes, as if he'd seen a horrible sight, were bulging and wide open and pure white like those of a pan seared trout.

From the looks of things, the man hadn't been dead long, as no land varmints or the birds had done him any real damage.

Studying the twisted body more closely, Ryker

noticed the flute clutched in the dead man's right hand—the ancient breastplate lay at his side partly concealed by the edge of the jacket he wore.

Dax must have been watching the farm, and seeing no one about, he'd taken the opportunity to raid the cavern and steal the artifacts. Whiskey Jim would declare the curse had killed the man, and based on what he saw, Ryker couldn't claim otherwise.

"Who is it?"

He glanced over his shoulder. Una had tied the donkey and gelding to a tree, and before he could stop her, she peered around him, then she gasped and clutched his arm. "Is that the man who shot at us near the cave? Saints preserve me, what happened to him?"

"Yes, it is, or rather was. And I'm not sure."

"What is he holding?" She reached out as if intending to retrieve the flute.

"Don't." Ryker grabbed her none too gently and held her back. "Those are the artifacts from your cave. You mustn't touch them."

She wretched free of his grasp and assumed a defiant stance, hands on her hips. "You were eager enough to be gettin' your hands on the ancient relics." Her voice sounded harsh and unnatural, and there was a wildness about her eyes while her normally generous lips flattened into a cruel line. A hedonistic desire flooded his senses, and the urge to hold the long-coveted items nearly overwhelmed him as well. A dangerous power had been set free and was at work here.

Not heeding his warning, Una pushed him aside and advanced toward the dead man.

Snagging the shawl from around her shoulders,

149

Ryker hurried forward to cover the sacred objects Dax had dared to steal. Una staggered backward, one hand to her head as if coming out of a trance. He too felt set free from the spell. One arm across her shoulders, he walked them both farther away from the ghastly scene.

Una faced him, her hands pressed against his chest, her gaze riveted on his face. "I'm sorry. Thank you for stopping me. I wasn't myself for a moment. I'd lost my commonsense, and not from being hit on the head."

From beneath her blouse, she retrieved a leather strap holding a pendent. The symbols resembled runes he'd seen in Scotland, and she clutched the necklace as if drawing comfort or protection from the engraved disc. "We must bury him and return the items to the cave."

"I agree. But without a shovel, the deed will be near impossible. Covering him with branches and rocks will have to suffice until I can return to do a proper job." Ryker had no fond feelings for Dax, but no man should be left to be torn apart by vultures and coyotes. "In the meantime, we need to get you and those relics back to the farm."

Without glancing at or touching the breastplate and flute, he gathered the items within the folds of the thick woolen shawl and set them aside. Then after following through with their plan of shielding the dead man's body as best they could, they headed to Una's place.

****

Unable to locate Whiskey Jim, who seemed to be an authority on the legend and relics, Ryker suggested leaving the artifacts in the cave—wrapped in Una's shawl—inside a sturdy wooden chest—secured with a chain and padlock. While they waited to figure out what to do next, Una kept watch at the farm for Whiskey, and Ryker went back to bury Dax Thompson.

Approaching the open space where they first found the body, he was surprised to find the turkey vultures nowhere in sight. When his horse came to an abrupt halt and refused to go any farther, Ryker dismounted and approached the pile of brush and rock on foot. Tossing aside the makeshift covering he stood back in stunned silence.

Dax's clothes and boots were still there, but his body was gone, turned to dust.

Chapter Sixteen

Una stood in the cave beside Ryker and Mr. Jim. The ginger root had calmed her stomach, and the blueberries had bolstered her strength. But as shadows danced across the walls in the muted glow of the kerosene lamp, the movement threatened to bring back the dizziness caused by her head injury.

She had never been inside the cave. The night Hamish had dared to sleep there, he had been greatly affected—and not in a good way. And he warned her to stay away. Becoming acquainted with Mr. Jim and learning the legend of Break Heart Canyon reinforced the warning to keep her distance.

Ryker ran his hand along the wall of the second chamber, which lay in partial ruins. "Dax used a heavy hand on the pickax to fulfill his contract with Mr. Cockrell. I'm guessing he didn't have time to send a telegram to our employer bragging about his success."

"I wouldn't say being turned to ash was much of a success story." Mr. Jim glanced around and shook his head as if saddened by the destruction.

"I'm glad what happened to him didnae happen to you, Ryker." She couldn't bear to think of seeing him in the same condition.

"Yes. Quite the sobering thought."

"I no longer believe you would steal the relics lying at your feet. Not anymore. After you saw the white panther, you'd decided not to disturb the artifacts."

Ryker studied her, surprised she had guessed correctly. "Maybe." He shrugged off the admission. "The question now is what do we do with the deadly objects?"

"The artifacts must be restored to the tomb and the wall again sealed." Mr. Jim stated the obvious.

"Oh, is that all? And how do you propose we manage that?" Ryker kicked at the wooden trunk. "We can't touch the flute or the breastplate, and you said we can't view the remains of the Indian Chief or the Shaman."

"I said a person with greed or evil intentions couldn't touch them or gaze upon the bones of the long dead. But a person with goodness in their heart, who honors the ways of the past, could right this wrong and bring comfort and peace to the two souls languishing here."

Both men turned to face her. Una took a step back. Since her arrival in America, she had been careful not to be seen holding rituals or making public her use of herbs and minerals. Knowing the downside of being discovered as a practitioner, she protected her beliefs.

In Scotland, her family had been shunned by those who did not understand the use of Nature for healing and living in harmony with the spiritual world. Her own brothers wanted nothing to do with her or to learn the long-forgotten arts. Several years older than she, they moved to the cities for work, never bothering to come back.

Even Hamish had been wary of her ways, refusing to learn from her or speak of what he considered pagan practices. After discovering her inclination toward the unusual, she'd been fortunate he'd taken her as his wife. The difference in their beliefs had always stood between them, yet often enough, their affection for one another had breached the gap.

"Don't be alarmed." Mr. Jim reached out and touched her shoulder, drawing her back into their circle of discussion as he led them all to the outer main chamber.

"Why would you suggest such a thing?" she asked as they moved toward the cave entrance.

"The elders of which I spoke showed me a world only a few are allowed to enter. And among many astounding revelations, they taught me the gift of seeing the color surrounding a person. There is a nimbus about our bodies. Each one unique in color, able to change and grow or recede in brightness. The basic hue rarely alters. You cannot hide what is in your heart. You know I speak the truth."

She'd heard of this phenomenon but had never acquired the ability. To see such things sounded a heavy responsibility and being able to do so explained how Mr. Jim knew where her beliefs rested.

She hazarded a glance at Ryker. How would he react to the fact she was an herbalist and practitioner of near forgotten lore?

His expression held expectancy, not condemnation. Were her special skills obvious to him as well? She should just wear a sign. Una caught MacTavish's eye as he sat just outside the entrance to the cave. "Either these two are smarter than they look, or we haven't been as canny as I thought." MacTavish whined and gave a sweet wolfish howl.

"Your special connection to the land and animals is hard to miss," Ryker admitted.

"I've no ken or heritage connected to this legend. I'm practiced in the traditions and ceremonies of my birth country not the Wild West." After what happened to Dax Thompson, she feared if anything went wrong, she would end up the same. "This is dangerous."

"Of course, it's up to you, Una." Was Mr. Jim giving her an out? "Unlike the fellow who was intent on defiling what was buried behind this wall, you would be setting matters in your canyon to right." No, she'd been wrong. He made amending the imbalance her responsibility, nay obligation.

"You are up to the task, Una. And isn't there a little part of you excited to delve into a world similar yet different from what you have seen before?"

He had her there. An opportunity to test her strength rarely came along. And wasn't this for a good cause? Yet she took a big chance revealing so blatantly the skills she worked many years to learn and hide.

Envisioning the surrounding land, her land, she realized Mother Nature lived here as deeply as in the soil of Scotland. If she were to thrive in Colorado, then honoring the earth from which she took sustenance was the only way to move forward.

"You've convinced me, but there is much preparation to be done before I can do what you ask."

The shoulders of both men seemed to slump in relief. Hers tightened, and their belief in her sent her anxiety up a notch.

"We'll need to wait until sundown." Old habits die hard. One never knew where prying eyes might be hiding. And spirits good or evil were more likely to appear in darkness.

Una hoped the love she felt for the canyon and valley would stand with her tonight. Even when Hamish had died on the jagged rocks, she never blamed the land. Would his spirit hover near tonight as well? She would need all the help she could get.

What worried her most was her ability to control the malevolence and unrest that had been unleashed. Granny Riona had raised her to give thanks to Mother Nature for benevolent help. She hadn't taught her how to fight a war against evil.

Rushing from the cave, she sought to be alone. Unaware of what was to come, MacTavish leaped about and ran in joyful circles. He seemed glad for her having exited the dark place he refused to enter. Perhaps the dog knew better than she did.

****

Following Una's lead, Ryker and Whiskey Jim stepped out into the light.

Maybe this wasn't such a good idea after all. But the die had been cast and Una had agreed of her own free will. The adventurous part of the spirited woman couldn't say no. Just as the adventurous part of Ryker had brought him here. And while he no longer had a purpose in Colorado, she did.

Mr. Cockrell would likely demand his seed money back, and there went his finder's fee and bonus. But no worries, another adventure could easily be found—if he cared to look. Feeling anchored to the mountains and prairie as if he were a ship having finally found home port, moving on had lost its appeal. And not just because of a pretty face and the desire he felt for Una.

Over the last few years, the need to belong had

grown in him—belong to a country, an ideal, a person, something. We all want someone to worry over us when we're late coming home at night.

Whiskey Jim broke in on his thoughts. "We'd better gather what's needed to make mortar if we plan on reconstructing the back wall when this is over."

Good idea. A little hard work sounded better than mulling over his past or second-guessing his future.

****

Locking the cabin door, Una stripped bare and approached the table holding the necessary articles for her invocations of protection. With her evening chores done, she had no excuse to forestall preparing for the ritual.

Never had she dealt with healing on such a grand scale. Offering prayers to save a kid goat or helping Kate with her baby was one thing, this was monumental. The spirits she faced tonight were old and bitter and powerful. Now released, they would be fearsome, lost, angry, and suffering.

Since she and Ryker brought the artifacts back to the cave, the birds had stopped singing and the animals in the holding pens huddled closer together. Wallace and The Countess kept watch, ears alert, tails twitching.

Laying out the only white garment she had to wear, Una touched the fine fabric and lace—her wedding dress would serve a new purpose. She must be focused and strong. Hamish was part of the land too, and she would wear the dress as much for him this time as the first. He and the land deserved to rest in peace—another reason to get this over and done.

Opening the ceramic jar, she gathered a precious handful of Celtic sea salt and pressed the sacred crystals to her forehead, between her breasts and at the apex of her thighs. With a white cloth soaked in water having been blessed during the last full moon, she squeezed the water over her head. The cold liquid trickled over her body as she chanted.

Mother Earth hear your daughter,
Cleanse me now with salt and water.
Cloak of courage and protection
Give me guidance and direction.
Banish darkness with this charm
Restore this land and do no harm

Without drying off, she stepped into the white dress, cinched up the waist, and pulling apart the seams of a pillowcase, she fashioned a white head covering. At the table, she sat and tugged on serviceable footwear, then she finished drinking the prepared tea of lavender, cinnamon, parsley, and cloves.

Gaining her feet, she reached for the necklace hanging on the back of the front door. Having removed the charm to bathe, she now slipped the cord of the amulet over her head, and for a moment, she held fast to the copper disc. Etched with the seal of Venus on a Friday at three o'clock, this was her personal protection. Would the talisman be strong enough to save both her mind and body as she battled whatever had been unleashed?

Retrieving the bag of goat hair and the sage smudge stick she'd prepared, she unlocked the door and ventured forth. Loyal MacTavish fell in step at her side and they made their way to the cave. The moon, shielded by a cloudy sky, struggled to light her way. No matter, she knew the path by heart.

Ryker and Mr. Jim met her at the entrance. Even

with the lantern turned down low, their grim expressions were readily visible. When she drew closer, Ryker sucked in a quick breath. "You look like an angel."

"I pray the real ones will be protectin' us from evil tonight."

"When first they were buried, madness and wickedness did rule," Mr. Jim agreed, "now you can give these two a chance to finally rest in peace."

Ryker reached for and clasped her hand, escorting her so elegantly you'd think they were stepping onto a dancefloor rather than entering a cave and the possibility of fighting for their lives.

They slipped through the fissure to the back chamber. Unchained, the trunk containing the flute and breastplate emanated a palpable force. She lit the smudge stick from the kerosene lamp. The purifying aroma permeated the cave, and breathing deep to bolster her courage, she directed the smoke over and around her body reinforcing her shield of protection.

"Has the tomb been prepared?" Once she dared to hold the artifacts, laying them to rest as quickly as possible was a priority.

"Yes." Ryker stepped aside so she could see the opening in the back wall. At the foot of the damaged area, the broken pieces along with new rocks were stacked beside a large bucket of what she guessed was mortar.

Arms wide, palms up, Una began to hum. Louder and louder, she lost herself to the vibration as the sound filled her body and reverberated off the walls of the cave. The thrumming in her chest felt like the wuthering on the Scottish moors. Chanting an old

Gaelic prayer Granny Riona entrusted to her years ago, she repeated the words three times, and her body became so light she no longer felt the earth beneath her feet

****

Dressed in white, her untamed red hair hidden, Ryker thought Una appeared fragile, but there was strength in the timbre of her voice as she hummed and uttered invocations he didn't understand. When the words she spoke stopped, the lid to the trunk burst open.

Ryker and Whiskey Jim jumped in surprise. Unwavering, Una held her ground. Drawing forth the wool roving from the bag she'd brought, she wrapped her hands in the mohair and reached for the breastplate. With care and respect, she elevated the artifact—offering the relic to the spirits. Unhindered by the rubble strewn across the floor, she entered the tomb area and carefully laid the artifact across the chest of the skeletal remains.

Holding the smoked amber glass used for the eclipse, Ryker and Whiskey dared to glance into the chamber. The bones of the ancient chief were unlike any Ryker had ever seen. Fossilized, they nearly glowed in their whiteness, and judging by the length of the femur, the person would have stood nearly eight feet tall.

Relative in size, and containing large threatening teeth, the skull was frightful to behold. A golden orb was clutched in the skeleton's right hand. Apparently even Dax had been too frightened to pry the bounty from the boney fingers.

Finished arranging the breastplate on the chest of

the chieftain, Una returned to collect the flute. As she did so, a rumbling from deep in the Earth shook the ground sending rocks and debris trickling down from the ceiling.

Fighting the urge to reach for Una to draw her to the safety of his embrace, Ryker balled his hands into fists. He may not understand what they were experiencing, but the chaos he felt swirling around them demanded they finish what they started—and it best be done in all haste.

Revering the flute, Una uttered more words Ryker couldn't interpret. He'd been pondering the material from which the flute was made. Then he'd recalled a picture Cockrell had shown him of a fossil discovered in a Texas cave nearly ten years ago. The Smilodon, affectionately called the saber tooth tiger, had roamed the area freely. Believing the flute had been carved from a fresh tooth of the ancient tiger meant the shaman and chief had lived thousands of years ago, before the dawn of modern man. Before the existence of the recent Indians once prolific in the West. And for the magic in the relic to endure for centuries gave claim to its power.

Cradling the flute in the protective goat hair, Una re-entered the burial chamber hastily placing the instrument on a mound of white bones which was covered with a piece of woven fabric. The flute immediately came alive emitting shrieking tones which flew through the air like solid objects.

Hands covering her ears, Una stumbled backward ending up in Ryker's arms. He held her upright, and along with Whiskey Jim, they managed the fissure to the main chamber and ran for the mouth of the cave. The cool evening air hit him like a slap across the face.

MacTavish howled at the sight of them.

The ground trembled, then shook violently. Rocks fell and tumbled about where once they stood inside the cave. Then the scream of a big cat echoed in the night, and startled they turned to face the canyon.

The snarling, growling, mournful sound chilled Ryker to the bone as he watched the image of the mystical white panther merged with Cougar Rock. Eyes wide, MacTavish wormed his way between Ryker and Una.

The noise ceased, suddenly and completely, and for a moment he feared he'd gone deaf. The unnerving stillness and crushing silence became suffocating, as if a woolen blanket had been tossed and staked down over the entire area. Then the leaves at his feet began to stir, swirling, dancing, tumbling higher and higher as a mighty wind thundered across the valley.

With their vision reduced to nothing amidst the dust and debris, the three of them swayed in the tempest and fought to remain upright. Una clung to Ryker, and Whiskey Jim had his arms around them both. The windstorm gathered force nearly tearing them apart. Una twisted her fingers in the fabric of his shirt, and the wind screamed like a human. Then the gale force disappeared up the canyon, and the unexpected cessation of movement had them stumbling backward to recover their footing.

Gulping in a much-needed breath, Ryker peered through the darkness steeling himself for Nature's next assault. When none came, he relaxed, and Una untangled herself from his embrace.

"That sure was a whoop and a holler." Whiskey Jim hooted and laughed, sounding as if he enjoyed the phenomenon. "I couldn't determine if the gods were angry or appeased by what we did."

"Only time will tell." Una hugged her dress closer as if fending off the cold uncertainty of what the outcome might be.

Ryker glanced toward the cave. "Before we call this a done deal, maybe we should take a gander inside and see what happened in there. Leaving the tomb open doesn't sound like a good idea."

The kerosene lantern was extinguished but unbroken. Upon relighting the lamp, the brightness hurt Ryker's eyes, and he barely made out the gigantic boulders completely blocking the rear chamber and burial vault. Unless they came armed with TNT, no one would ever desecrate the tomb again.

Chapter Seventeen

Spending the night with Una had been Ryker's first impulse, but he knew instinctively doing so was not a wise decision. She'd been exhausted and nearly incoherent. He'd yet to compromise a fair lady without first gaining her permission, and he didn't plan on starting now. So after chasing down his horse, which had bolted in fear during the maelstrom, he'd returned to and spent what was left of the night in Cañon City.

Knowing Whiskey Jim watched over Una, Ryker felt she would be safe and well cared for. And there were things in town needing his attention. Top of the list was making the cattlemen pay for terrorizing Una and trying to burn down her farm.

Before he'd found her with the moonshiners, a fright he'd never before encountered struck him like a shot of Toas lighting. Having fought in wars, he'd been scared before, afraid he might die. But he'd never panicked at the possibility of another person losing their life. The incident had torn down the wall he'd built around his heart as easily as Dax had torn down the wall in the cave. Both walls built long ago but not forgotten. Perhaps removing his was long overdue. And all because of his meeting Una MacLaren.

Which brought him back around to seeing justice done for the way she'd been treated. Last night he'd considered hanging out at the saloon where the rough necks from the cattle ranch frequented, but he'd also been drained and off kilter after what the three of them had gone through. So after sending a telegram to Mr. Cockrell vaguely depicting the latest developments, he'd hit the hay. The men would be easy enough to find another time.

This morning as he finished his breakfast in the hotel restaurant, he wracked his brain for a suitable plan of retribution. Going to the law was no good. In this town, the law and justice were two different things. Whiskey had informed him the sheriff was cousin to the man who ran large cattle company responsible. Badge or no badge, the man would never take sides against family.

Ryker was about to leave the restaurant when two gentlemen entered and sat at the table nearest the window. He wasn't privy to their conversation and hadn't seen them before in town. The eclipse observers and curiosity seekers being long gone, who could they be? Well-dressed and cleanshaven, they appeared men of means. They both wore sidearms.

Polly, the easy-on-the-eyes waitress at the eatery, took their order. A few minutes later she reappeared with a coffee pot and after serving the two men, she swung by his table to refill his cup as well.

"Say, Polly, do you know who those men are?"

"Revenuers." Her tone barely hid her dislike.

"Are you sure?" The men in the forest who had taken care of Una came to mind. If they were caught distilling liquor, they could go to jail and be heavily fined for not paying taxes.

"I'm sure," she nodded. "I heard them bragging at supper last night about a bunch of moonshiners they rounded up down in Pueblo. They seem a determined pair. Anxious for more notches on their belt if you get my drift."

Not many people had a soft spot for tax collectors.

"Then they're not just passing through on the way to Denver."

"They don't seem in a hurry to leave."

As he considered her response, Cookie called for Polly to retrieve the order for the men they were discussing. "Gotta run. Anything else I can get for ya?"

"No, I'm good. Thank you."

She spun around and hurried off.

This information might hold promise. What exactly, he couldn't say. Ideas dragged through his mind like anchors, but none grabbed hold or held tight. He also had personal troubles to mull over. Before breakfast, he'd checked in at the telegraph office. A reply from Mr. Cockrell had been waiting for him. Far from happy, the man seemed more distressed about the loss of his trophy than the death of Dax. And to Ryker's surprise, his employer indicated he was heading for Cañon City.

Ryker rose to his feet, left money on the table, and sauntered past the revenuers. As unobtrusively as possible, he scrutinized the men so he wouldn't forget their faces. Out on the boardwalk, he stopped short, nearly running into Whisky Jim.

"What are you doing in town? Is Una all right?" Glancing up and down the street, he half expected to see her pink pony cart and Wallace's big ears.

"She's at the farm. She kicked me out this morning, claiming she needed time alone to gather her strength in the ways she knew best. As I left, I smelled that smudge stick of hers going full blast. She's got her own method of doing things. If she didn't, last night would not have been successful. I don't ask questions. It's her business. Just like my way of doing things is my business."

Jim's tone told Ryker to back off and settle down.

"Are you aware there are Federal tax collectors in town?"

"I heard tell. Their presence bodes ill for the boys down yonder."

"I had the same concern. We should alert them."

"I have a feeling they're aware. Such news travels fast in their circle."

"What do you know about the Pritchard ranch?"

At the quick change of subject, Whiskey Jim came to attention and his eyes narrowed. "I know they didn't get to be the biggest cattle conglomerate around by playing fair."

"They deserve payback."

"If you figure out how, I'd be interested. In the meantime, I'm off on my errands for the man on the hill."

"You're talking about the place you can see from Una's, right. What's that all about?"

"An old man lives there. I do odd jobs for him and pick up what he needs from town."

"Why is he so secretive?"

"Not secretive. He just likes to keep to himself. After a terrible grievous event, he holed up, and he enjoys his peace and anonymity."

"Sounds like you understand him quite well."

"Do we ever truly understand another person? The human spirit, while strong, is malleable. And hearts are easily swayed by good and evil, especially where greed is concerned. Remember what happened to Dax Thompson."

"I see you're on one of your philosophical benders today. But I agree the lure of money was his undoing."

Whiskey Jim gave a chuckle. "I guess I am waxing poetic. And I'm late for an appointment with Jordie Millbrook at the bank. He and Kate are a nice young couple."

"How's the baby doing?"

"Very well from all accounts. As is the mother."

"Thanks to Una."

"Yes. Mrs. MacLaren has a good heart. A steadfast heart. And hers won't easily be swayed. At least not by riches."

As Whiskey Jim headed for the bank, Ryker was sure this last bit of information was directed at him personally. His relationship with Jim had changed, and they seemed more comfortable around one another. Shared experiences demanding trust and courage affected relationships with the people involved. Did this mean Whiskey was more accepting of Ryker's feelings for Una?

Last night, while lying in bed, dog tired but unable to sleep, he'd decided to stick around Colorado, or more specifically, take residence close to Una. This was a huge departure from his usual way of thinking, and the idea of keeping his boots in one place for any length of time made him sweat. The scary part was the notion didn't seem a passing fancy. His feet sought more secure footing—steadfast not foot loose.

But first things first.

****

Una sat in the sun soaking up the heat, trying to renew her vigor and strength, which had been sucked out of her during the ceremony. She felt thin, as if the breeze could flow through her body.

The smudge stick ritual would ensure no malicious entities clung to her mind or spirit. And to be honest, she'd felt no evil swirling around in the dark chaos, only devastating grief, guilt, and the need for repentance. Although the legend for which her canyon was named would always endure, she hoped the spirits of the shaman and the chief had found solace.

The story of the young lovers from centuries ago had always seemed intertwined with her sorrow in losing Hamish. But lately, she was changing. With his attention, humor, and willingness to help, Ryker Landry softened the pain. To be honest he seemed to soften her whole world—easing her grip on the past, allowing her to reach for the future.

She couldn't help but have womanly feelings for Ryker. But if his presence turned out to be fleeting, would a moment in time be enough? To again feel the caress of a hand and the whisper of a kiss was a huge temptation, golden moments as precious to her as any treasure.

As if to see how she faired today, Wallace and The Countess ambled over and stood beside her. Reaching out, she gave each velvety muzzle a stroke. "Thank you for being steadfast during the riotous doings last night. I knew I could count on you to keep the goats calm." Head bobs and huffing said *you're welcome*.

Una gained her feet and leaned against The Countess. "I'm tired." Her words floated out on a whisper, and she realized her heart and soul were as weary as her body. "Making all the decisions on my own is taking its toll. And as much as I love you wonderful beasts, on occasion I'm lonely. My own fault, or so Kate reminds me. Perhaps she's correct. Maybe it's time I opened my heart to more than four-legged beings." The renewed huffing and head bobs showed total agreement.

Soon winter would sweep down their valley, and the Farmer's Almanac predicted lots of snow and lots of cold. Winter was the worst time to be alone, regrets and fears often seemed more real as she spun baskets of mohair and listened to the hungry coyotes on the hunt.

At least, Wallace would have The Countess to help him protect the goats, another comfort as she worried about him being hurt trying to save the tribe singlehandedly. You're my biggest baby, aren't ye, girl, and I see you've rolled in the nearby dust patch. Brushing leaves and bits of dry grass from the jenny's mane, she wondered what Ryker was doing today.

Finally surrendering to the thoughts he inspired, she had begun to enjoy them. In the cave, she'd felt his protectiveness and couldn't have gone through the ordeal without relying on him to defend her. He hadn't turned away from or showed fear of the things she knew and the words she'd spoken. Of course, she couldn't imagine many things would strike fear in the heart of Ryker Landry.

Recalling the scoured fleece she'd left soaking in the alum water, she passed through the gate to the outdoor washstand. After examining a handful of hair, she decided only one more rinse was needed before she could spread the mohair across the wirecloth. Once dried on the wooden frame, she must decide whether to make roving for spinning or hair for felting. The mittens for the school children could be made from either. Felting would be quicker and utilize parts of the hair bundle less suitable for spinning.

Shaking the water from her hands, she dried them on her apron on the way to the shed to check on supplies. The coffee grounds and onion skins, marigolds, Queen Anne's lace, and red cabbage were ready and waiting to be used to dye the mohair. For deep brown, bright yellow, and blue, she traded her finished items for walnuts, turmeric, and woad. The dying process was demanding, but the results were inspiring and often unexpected.

Spinning and weaving comforted her, reminding her of Scotland and Granny Riona—a world away and a lifetime ago. Una had stayed with Granny Riona until she left this Earth, and the house she grew up in was taken by the tax collectors. Which was why owning the farm free and clear in this wild Colorado meant security and peace of mind to her. But only if she figured out what to do about the cattlemen.

Who could she hire for protection? Ryker was a soldier of fortune. Why not him? But he would expect recompense and she had little to offer monetarily. Or maybe Mr. Jim knew of a trustworthy person for the job.

She glanced at the house on the hill. Although secretive, the old man who lived there had a generous heart. He'd donated money when a new roof was needed for the schoolhouse where Kate taught. And when hardships turned desperate, a family often found a basket of food or clothing sent their way. Delivered by Mr. Jim, figuring out from whence they came was easy enough.

The impressive house oozed Victorian charm with gingerbread on every peak and turret. And even the old timers in the area couldn't remember when the house did not stand sentry over her valley. She'd been tempted a time or two to sneak up the hill and peek in the windows, to verify if the inside was as impressive as the outside. But she treasured her seclusion and wouldn't dream of invading the owner's privacy.

Only one other abode in the area surpassed such grandeur—Silas Pritchard's place, or Boss Pritchard. She'd only heard about the ranch and was happy to keep a river between her and the cattle king. The man seemed determined to see her driven from her land—or dead. Whichever came first.

Chapter Eighteen

The flyers hanging on every post in town held a message as pompous as the man who'd commissioned them to be tacked up.

Cattleman's Ball
Saturday August 17th.
$100 per couple.
7P.M.—until the cows come home.
Enquire at Fremont bank.

Ryker tore down the handbill attached to the striped barber shop pole.

Rich as Midas, Boss Pritchard still had the audacity to charge people to come to his party. Or maybe making folks pay was his way of keeping out the less well-heeled individuals who made up most of the town. Either way, the dinner party seemed a golden opportunity to serve this puffed-up prairie chicken his well-deserved comeuppance.

Crossing the street, Ryker crumpled the paper and tossed the notice onto a pile of horse dung. Pritchard's highfalutin status, and his believing he was better than his peers, seemed vital to the man. Therefore, to sully his reputation at the party in front of the town's most influential people would cut deep. An idea came to mind, but he was going to need Whiskey Jim's help.

Waiting for Whiskey to finish his business at the bank, Ryker amused himself by checking the notices tacked up in the telegraph office window. Mr. Cockrell's recent communique had stated he would be arriving in a day or two. Why was his employer coming here at all? He could fire Ryker's caboose easy enough by wire. And if Cockrell wanted the advance money returned, Ryker would figure a way to come up with the cash to wire back. He'd work for the money or sell something, although he had few items of value other than the geode. Una's geode. No way he was parting with that connection to her.

Ambling back the way he'd come, Ryker noticed Jordie personally escorting Whiskey Jim out of the bank. Despite his down-trodden appearance and unassuming ways, Whiskey garnered respect in town, partly because he worked for the man on the hill and partly because he'd earned the accolade himself.

"Morning, Jordie," he called, quickening his pace as the two men shook hands in parting.

"Good morning, Ryker. Ready to invest in our community and settle down?"

The question didn't inspire the usual panic and gastric distress. "Your suggestion isn't as outrageous a notion as I once would have thought."

"Glad to hear it." Jordie chuckled. Whiskey gave Ryker a curious glance.

"Today, however, I'm on a mission of making money not investing money. Anybody around here in need of temporary help for hire? I'm good with horses and hammers."

"As a matter of fact, Kate has several projects at the school house crying for attention. There's a loose railing on the porch, and one of the walls needs a new support. The wind last winter piled a ton of snow against the north side, and now it's listing a bit."

"Okay if I drop by today and enquire if I can be of service?"

"I don't see why not. Kate should be around preparing for the fall school season. I think she finds more joy in the first day of school then the children, and she'll probably have a large list of chores for you."

"Sounds good."

"Well, gentlemen, I'd better get back to work." Jordie nodded good bye, and held the door for an approaching customer, then he followed the man into the bank.

"Whiskey, if you've got a minute, I have a situation I need to discuss with you."

"I'm always up for coffee at the hotel restaurant."

****

Gaining the older man's consensus for causing a ruckus at the Cattlemen's Ball hadn't taken as much persuading as Ryker had figured. Whiskey's main objection was his concern the incident might make things worse for Una rather than better. A possibility. But not showing the willingness to fight back also sent a message—defeat and easy pickin's.

Besides, Ryker had come to a decision. He didn't plan to hit and run, he intended to stay around and protect Una and her farm. He also suggested they enlist the aid of the man on the hill. Whiskey seemed to have an in with the fellow. If the highly respected resident took an interest and cast his influence their way, the townspeople would take note. They didn't know how his support might come in handy.

On his way to the schoolhouse, the ingenious plan ran through his mind. Counter reasons as to why things could go horribly wrong also occurred to him. Also, giving the man a taste of his own medicine would be especially hard when the *patient* was surrounded by his bodyguards.

"Hello at the schoolhouse." As he approached, Ryker called out a greeting so as not to startle Kate.

She came to the door cuddling her pink-cheeked baby boy in her arms. "Mr. Landry. What are you doing here? Would you like to register for the fall classes?"

"No doubt with you as schoolmarm, learning would be a treat, but actually I'm here looking for work. I saw Jordie in town, and he said you could use a hand with a few repairs."

"How fortunate for me. Please come through, and I'll make you out a list."

Fingers crossed, he willed there would be enough chores to result in part of the hundred dollars he needed to attend Boss Pritchard's party.

Inside, Kate set the baby on a blanket spread out in a corner. Two chairs, turned on their sides, formed a barrier keeping him in place as he played with a homemade wooden rattle.

The smell of wood polish and freshly sharpened pencils drifted around the big sunlit room, and memories of his own childhood struggled for his attention. While his parents were alive, he'd attended school, thankfully learning to read and write. Then upon their untimely death he'd been farmed out to relatives who put more credence in using his body rather than his brain. Their plan backfired. The hard labor made him strong, and he struck out on his own as soon as he was able. Since that day, no man told him when or where to put his back to use.

As Kate handed Ryker the list, a small boy ran inside nearly colliding with the both of them. "Mrs. Millbrook, I brung the clothes my momma promised you. The ones for the baby. I out growed them years and years ago." He handed her a bundle wrapped in a clean feed sack.

"Why thank you, Billy. They'll be put to good use. The clothes are a kind and generous gift." She set the bundle aside. "Remember next time to say you brought the clothes, not brung them. And you outgrew them not out growed them. Saying those sentences correctly would be like another gift for me."

"I'll done get the words right next time, ma'am."

Her expression went from amused to alarmed when the lad wiped his hand on the thigh of his pants leaving a small streak of blood,

"Oh, little one, what happened to you?"

"I got cut on the railing out front when I was a comin' up the steps."

"Mr. Landry, sanding down and securing the wooden balustrade is now at the top of our list of repairs." Grabbing a leather pouch from the side desk drawer, Kate led Billy around Ryker and outside to the pump. Retrieving a bar of soap from the pouch she washed the boy's hand, and holding an impressively large pair of tweezers, she commenced inspecting the wound for splinters. The boy blanched but didn't whine or pull his hand away.

Noticing the absence of his mother, the baby began to squall and fuss. Ryker waited at the door for Kate to return. Instead, she called to him over her shoulder.

"If you'd be so kind, Mr. Landry. See what little Jedidiah needs."

Approaching the corner with caution, he peered down at the scarlet-faced infant. "Howdy, young man. What seems to be the trouble?" The only response was an increase in the earsplitting sound. How could it be coming from such a small human being?

Ryker was impartial regarding children. If pushed, he'd probably admit he didn't particularly care for them. This attitude grew mostly from his lack of close contact with any. But now, seeing no other option, he reached down, firmly grasped the baby, and plucked him from his small prison. Arching and struggling, arms and legs waving, the distressed infant was more difficult to hold than a terrified jackrabbit.

Clasping the writhing baby to his chest, Ryker walked around the schoolroom in an attempt to calm the baby. Seeing this was not working, he loped back and forth in an attempt at amusement. When he realized the absurdity of the situation, he roared with laughter and Jedidiah followed suit gurgling with mirth. Grubby little hands reached up to tug at his ear and his hair. Ryker's hat canted sideways nearly tumbling to the floor. Not daring to stop and right his headgear, he continued to gallop around the room.

"Now there's a sight I'd never have predicted."

Ryker turned toward the door and Una's voice.

****

Seeing him holding Kate's baby melted a little more of her heart where her feelings for this man were concerned. "Have you added babysitting to your list of skills?"

"Definitely not."

As she stepped farther into the schoolroom, he hurried over and deposited the infant in her arms. Then he realigned his hat and wiped a bit of drool from his cheek. "I stopped by to help with repairs and was pressed into service."

"The babe seemed happy wrapped in your arms." Una would be too. "Safe and warm." Her last words slipped out unintended and especially not meant to be heard with such emotion. Heat flooded her cheeks. An unstoppable blush was sure to follow giving away her desire to also be held in this man's arms.

Ryker hadn't heard or pretended not to have notice her slip up. "Whiskey said you were recuperating at the farm. What brought you here?"

"I was restless and wanted an excuse to visit my friend Kate. And I came to find out how many children will be attending school this year. I need the number and ages as I plan to make mittens for each of them for the Christmas festival."

"A generous notion."

"More a necessity. I made woolen caps for them last year, and noticed most of the children's mittens had holes, or they'd outgrown them, or they didn't have any at all."

"I suppose you like kids."

"Some of them. I'm sure you were an abominable little boy."

"I don't doubt there are folks who would wholeheartedly agree with you."

Una rocked Kate's baby, enjoying the experience. She'd wanted children, and she and Hamish had tried—when Hamish felt like it. Quick and dutiful, she'd never call what they did making love. Maybe the lack of fire

179

between them was why there hadn't been any babies. Would being with Ryker be different?

Jedediah yanked a fistful of her hair, giving her a start. How long had she been staring at Ryker while these lusty visions tramped through her mind? She needed to snap to attention and stop daydreaming.

"So, everything is quiet out at the farm?"

"Yes. Today all is calm, but I feel I mustn't tarry when I'm away. And since you appear to be seeking employment—other than raiding caves, disturbing bones, and scoffing at legends—there's a question I've been meaning to ask you. I was wondering if I might hire you to protect my property."

There, she'd done it. She'd invited the man who disturbed her dreams to fill her days with sideways glances and heart palpitating nearness. She was playing with fire—and the heat warmed her to the core.

"Staying in town and riding back and forth would be a problem, especially if the cattlemen decide to strike at night. Is there no room in your cabin to accommodate me?" A twinkle in his eyes said staying in her bed sounded a good alternative.

"The barn is quite comfortable. And at present, there's a nanny and kid residing there to keep you jolly company."

A sputtering laugh was his first response. "You're serious, aren't you?"

She nodded, refusing to budge on the matter.

"All right. Regardless of the disappointing accommodations, I accept. But as long as the weather holds, camping out will suit me fine if you promise me a decent breakfast every morning."

"That's all I can promise until I sell my goods"

"Yet here you are intending to give your merchandise away. That's hardly good business sense."

"Regardless of cost, we must do things good for the soul."

He gave a little sniff of sarcastic amusement as if he'd expected such a response. "Then breakfast will do for now. I've always been one to trust to the future."

"Have you? Of late, my faith in what will come to pass seems a bit muddled and on the dark side." Wishing she hadn't exposed her views so readily, Una nuzzled the crook of the baby's neck, eliciting a squeal of delight from the child.

"The path is brighter if the person at your side holds a lamp to light the way."

His remark struck deep, and again she realized she and Hamish had never reached that plateau. Despite sharing the cabin and kitchen table, at times she'd felt like the hired help rather than a partner. What a joy and comfort to journey through life as an unbeatable team facing all difficulties hand in hand—and winning.

Did she detect another side to this mercenary besides his desire of money and adventure? An appreciation for simple things also seemed to reside within him. Or perhaps these ideas were just fanciful and much needed reassurance on her part, because not giving her heart to this man was becoming more and more of a challenge.

"Do try to keep the bandage clean, Billy. At least for one day." Kate called the advice to the little boy scrambling off into the underbrush on the trail of the weasel he'd spotted. Then Una's friend came running up the schoolhouse steps.

"Una, how wonderful to see you." Setting aside the

leather kit, Kate opened her arms to receive the baby struggling to reach her.

"Kate, Jedediah has grown so much."

"Yes, we're both in fine fettle." She glanced back and forth between Una and Ryker and they both took a step back from one another. "Have I interrupted something?" Her raised brows indicated she hoped so.

"No." Spoken in unison and loudly, the tiny word felt more like a yes.

Even the baby laughed as if he knew they weren't telling the truth.

Ryker navigated around the women and headed for the door. "Have you a tool bin about the place? I'd best see to the loose and dangerous railing."

"Around back," Kate directed.

"I didn't realize Mr. Landry would be here." Why did she feel the need to explain her reason for running into him?

Kate sat in a nearby chair and draping her shoulder with the lap blanket Una had made for her last Christmas, she began breast feeding her son. "He's a noticeably handsome man."

"Distressingly so." Una perched on the edge of the desk, apparently there was no avoiding the subject. "I confess he brings out an unnamed force within me, a force to which surrender is inevitable. These feelings are so different, Kate, not like when I was married. They make me hungry, and guilty, and frightened."

"Life is too short for unfounded guilt. Hamish would want you to be happy. He was the reason you came to this country. Maybe Mr. Landry is the reason you will continue to thrive here. Good or bad, people come into our lives for a reason. And they can abruptly leave when their reason has been fulfilled."

"A neat and tidy theory to explain away what Fate throws at us. But I will admit the man intrigues, annoys, and unsettles me. He's hinted at wanting to be more than just friends. And despite his reason for coming here not working out, as of yet he hasn't taken off like I imagined he would."

"Then give what could be a chance," Kate encouraged. "I love you, and I don't want you to be lonely."

"Being alone doesn't mean I'm lonely. In fact, I find myself rather good company."

"Of course you are, dear Una." Kate laughed and the baby hiccoughed. "But you know what I mean."

"Yes, I do. And I would enjoy someone with whom to share the sunny days, and gloomy storms, and especially the cold winter nights." They both giggled as that idea took shape in their minds.

"Obviously, he has a stalwart heart. Yet I'm not sure he can overcome his propensity for roaming faraway places." What if she offered her love to Ryker and he laughed, or left on the next train? At the very least, another sad tale would be added to the legend of Break Heart Canyon.

Chapter Nineteen

Ryker edged closer to the fire and poured another cup of morning coffee. Unsure of what Una would make for breakfast, coffee would at least get him going and warm him up. The temperatures last evening had dropped quickly after dark.

For his first night as Una's hired man, Ryker stayed at the old camp site by the cave. Ringed with stones, the firepit still stood and the brush had not grown near enough to cause worry.

He'd spent a restless evening, partly because of what had happened in the nearby cave, but mostly because he couldn't get Una MacLaren out of his mind. For the first time in his life, a woman not physically present in his bed kept him up at night. The vote was out on whether or not he liked the situation.

Dashing the dregs of coffee from his cup into the smoldering fire, he followed up dowsing the fire with what was left in the pot and the wash bucket. Enough soul searching. Time to go check the fence on the hill, the one that had previously been cut.

Finding all secure and having waited a suitable amount of time after sunrise, he decided to circle around to Una's cabin.

Not seeing her out and about, he grabbed the ax and began splitting the stack of cut wood. The thunk, thunk, thunk, of his labors echoed in the stillness of the morning.

The cabin door opened, and Una stepped out. "I won't pay you extra for doing more than riding the fence line and being available at night."

"Don't worry. This won't interfere with my regular rounds and making sure the perimeter is secure. Besides, it's good for me to be seen around the place giving these no-accounts pause for consideration before instigating more trouble. As far as being available at night… My evening skills are upon request and limited only by your imagination."

She seemed neither shocked nor put off by his insinuation, a good sign, right? Then she crooked a finger for him to follow as she returned to the cabin. Slamming the ax into a log, he dusted the woodchips from his hands and hurried after her.

Collecting a fork and the plate of food warming by the woodstove, she shoved both into his hands.

Eggs, berries, and mashed sweet potatoes—the offering made his mouth water. Without Una indicating he should sit at the table, Ryker respectfully retired to the stump by the front door. Before he'd downed two yummy mouthfuls, he noticed Wallace and The Countess snorting and fussing near the pasture gate. Ears on the alert, they stared off toward the edge of the property and sure enough a plume of trail dust began to rise above the far trees. MacTavish bristled and the cat padded over to a safer observation post in a clump of wild chamomile.

Figuring whoever approached intended no harm or they wouldn't be using the road, Ryker took time to savor more of his meal. He was hungry and had no intentions of being rushed.

When their visitor arrived and turned out to be Mr. Cockrell, the food roiled in his belly, and he wished he'd eaten less. The man bounced so vigorously atop the horse, to watch him was painful. Apparently riding a leather chair in his library was more familiar to him than riding a leather saddle.

Ryker handed the plate to Una. "It's the man who hired me to find the artifacts."

She stiffened and disappeared into the cabin, returning with her rifle—MacTavish at her side.

Ambling forward, Ryker caught the bridle of the horse, keeping his boss several paces back from the cabin. Dressed in tweeds and fancy clothes, the man appeared overheated and discombobulated.

"Thank goodness I found you." Uninvited, he slid to the ground and mopped his head with a big white handkerchief. "When folks out here say just down the road, they mean half a day's ride. I've never seen such wide-open spaces. Luckily, I ran into an old man hiking who gave me directions.

No doubt Whiskey Jim was the man to whom Cockrell referred. Should he thank or disparage his friend? But this inevitable face to face with his ex-employer had to happen sooner or later—might as well be now.

"The lady holding a rifle on you is Mrs. MacLaren, and you're trespassing on private land." Right on cue, MacTavish growled backing up Ryker's words

Cockrell glanced up, and his eyes widened as if he'd just noticed Una and the beast. "I heard folks out West were congenial and welcoming."

"They're also respectful of other people's property." Unless they were cattlemen, Ryker silently added.

Doffing his hat, Mr. Cockrell remembered his big city manners. "I apologize for my unannounced arrival, madam."

"Your unannounced departure would be more welcome." Una edged the barrel of the rifle off to one side yet kept the weapon at the ready. "There's noothin' of interest for the likes of you here."

"On the contrary. Here lives the opportunity to test a man's mettle. I've always paid men like Landry to search the far corners of the world for trophies to satisfy my amusement. And while my home is filled with remarkable objects, I am no longer entertained. I wanted to experience the adventure myself."

So living vicariously no longer filled the bill. Ryker hadn't seen this coming. What had prompted such a rash change in attitude? West of the Mississippi, the danger could be real and more than bargained for by someone with this naïve attitude. "You might find things here more exciting than you imagined."

"The blame lies with Stanley and his book, *How I Found Livingstone*. His tales of daring-do have become the talk of the town. Being all the rage with men in my circle, we've formed an Adventure Club. We each declare in writing the escapade we intend to take and the date by which it will be accomplished. There is speculation placed on each man's success, if you get my drift. And should anyone renege on going or fail to complete his quest, he loses the money he's posted plus any profit from wagers.

"I chose to come here to explore the Wild West."

Never in a hundred years had Ryker envisioned the chubby, out-of-shape little man leaving the comfort of his well-appointed home. But again, money and reputation appeared to be his motivation.

"One of the members got caught up in the *Tom Sawyer* illusion. The fellow went down the river on a raft and drowned. The loser became a hero posthumously, and the man who bet he'd never survive became rich." Cockrell laughed about the incident, leaving Ryker at a loss for words.

"But enough about the machinations of the rich back East." A snooty expression slipped into place on Cockrell's face as the man scrutinized Ryker from head to toe. Then he glanced around the farm. "Since you have failed at your undertaking, I had hoped to collect the advanced owed me. But by all appearances, I see this may not be fast in coming, if at all."

Ryker cringed inside, embarrassed for Una to hear he was down and out. "A temporary condition, I assure you. And I always pay my debts, monetarily—and otherwise."

This seemed to give Mr. Cockrell pause. "Yes, well, we can make arrangements. I'll be getting nothing back from Dax Thompson. Poor devil. The circumstances of his death were rather sketchy. I'd like more details as to what happened."

Again, his ex-employer seemed curious rather than sorry for the man's passing. "I'll be glad to fill you in, but this is neither the time nor place." Una stepped closer to Ryker as if to warn him not to tell what they had been through. "Besides, there isn't much I can add to what you already know." Her stance eased. He would always protect her, and not just from the cattlemen.

"I had to shell out a goodly sum to cover wagers when Dax's death came to light. The side bets had you more likely to die than Jax. Now you have both failed. Luckily, you mentioned the earthquake inside the cave. Considered an unavoidable act of Nature, I was off the hook for your disastrous attempt, and didn't lose any more money."

Ryker bristled at the man's lack of humanity in laying bets on his and Dax's success or demise, but no use causing a scene on Una's property. Besides, Ryker was glad things had turned out the way they had regarding the relics. And he couldn't be more delighted his ex-employer had gotten hit where it hurts, in the bank account.

Cockrell sighed, stretched, then massaged his lower back with one hand. "I don't suppose there are any places to let around here other than the hotel in town. The beds there are most uncomfortable, and the sheets, although clean, are quite worn."

"I may have a suggestion." Whiskey Jim appeared, startling all three of them.

"That's the stranger I passed on the road. To what do you allude, sir?"

Ryker wondered the same thing.

"I may be able to gain permission for you to stay at the house on the hill."

Mr. Cockrell's gaze switched to the residence mentioned. Whiskey sidled closer to Una and Ryker and spoke in hushed tones from the side of his mouth. "When we met on the road, he asked about the cattlemen party and Boss Pritchard. Better to keep an eye on him here. Don't need him hooking up with our enemy."

The idea made sense. Pritchard and Cockrell were cut from the same bolt of cloth, taking what they wanted regardless of who or what stood in their path. But Whiskey was making a pretty bold offer.

"I accept. Let us proceed immediately." Cockrell gathered the reins of his horse. "If someone would just give me a boost up, we can be off. We'll speak later, Mr. Landry, regarding payment."

With a wink at Ryker, Jim vigorously gave Mr. Cockrell a leg-up, nearly sending him up and over the saddle. Hat askew and huffing and puffing with indignation, the man clung to the horse's neck, looking like a horse's ass. "A little less enthusiasm would be appreciated, my good man."

Whiskey led the way, and Una rested the rifle at her side. "What a most disagreeable sort." As if to say good riddance as well, MacTavish turned his backside to the disappearing figures and scratched up dirt with his back feet. "I'm surprised Mr. Jim befriended him."

"I imagine Whiskey has a plan. I'm just concerned he would make such an offer without first checking with the owner."

"I hope he doesn't get into trouble. Now I'd best be gettin' the goats to the south pasture for their noon graze. They look ready to burst through the gate on their own."

"Want to go to the cattlemen's party?"

"I'll have noothin' to do with that horrible man."

"Kate and Jordie will probably be there."

"Kate and Jordie?"

"It's only good business for Jordie to fraternize with the bank's biggest customer. After all, The Fremont is overseeing the selling of the tickets.

"Say you'll come. At least there will be two nice people there to talk too, and they'll probably be glad to see us as well."

"I don't have the money for a ticket. And from the sounds of things neither do you."

"This is true, but not your concern. Do you want to go?"

"I've nothing fancy enough to wear to such an event."

"What about the dress you wore on our infamous doings in the cave."

"Not my poor wedding dress. It's been through enough. I cannae do it. I'll not be seen wearing it in the house of my bitter enemy."

"We'll figure something out, because I'll not take no for an answer."

Chapter Twenty

The night of the party broke clear and warm and wonderful. Then why were her hands cold as ice and her heart pounding like a terrible omen for what was to come?

Una stood beside Ryker at the grand front door to Boss Pritchard's grand estate. The burly wrangler barring their passage and demanding to see their invitation was one of the men who had tried to burn down her farm.

After verifying their ticket stubs, the ruffian moved aside, barely enough for them to squeeze by. "I'll be watching you two." He growled out the threat for only them to hear.

As if to respond, Ryker hesitated and stiffened at her side. She didn't blame him, she wanted to do the man a bit of harm herself. Rising above the challenge, and keeping calm, Ryker gently cupped her elbow and escorted her through the foyer and into the main room.

They shouldn't be doing this. Only trouble could be had in this explosive situation. But even Mr. Jim agreed the time had come for a showdown—and she truly was weary of living in fear for her animals and herself. She appreciated her friends wanting to secure her a more peaceful existence, but something warned her more than just her agenda would be unfolding tonight.

Nearly all the faces in the room belonged to friends of their host. And oh, there was Mr. Cockrell. Laughing and carrying on like a debutante wanting to be seen with the richest most powerful man in the county. The man made a spectacle of himself as he fluttered around Boss Pritchard.

Then as Ryker had predicted, she spotted Kate and Jordie standing in a quiet corner. A modicum of joy eased Una's trepidation. After tugging on Ryker's sleeve and nodding in their friends' direction, they set off to join the couple.

Being a schoolteacher and an assistant banker, they held loftier positions in the town hierarchy than did she—a goat farmer with dirt on her hands on a daily basis. But they called her friend and that meant a lot. Which was more than she could say for several of the town's people. The conspicuous glares fired her way by the group of ladies near the open French doors illustrated her point.

"Una, Ryker, I can't believe you dared to come." Kate reached for Una and hugged her. "A few moments ago, I made the mistake of asking the other women if they'd seen you. I got a curt no and was frozen out of the conversation. All these people are friends of or in cahoots with Boss Pritchard. They've taken sides. Your being here could be dangerous."

Una agreed. Ryker captured her hand and drew her closer. "Our not being here could be dangerous as well. We can't cower in the weeds waiting for their next attack. They need to realize we're willing to fight back."

His using the term *we* gave Una a thrill. Did Ryker see them as a couple? Her heart responded to the idea with a deliciously cozy feeling. Her brain continued to warn her to beware.

"Come along," Jordie suggested to Ryker. "Let's get the ladies a glass of punch."

And Una imagined, stronger libation for themselves.

When they were alone, Kate touched a ruffle on the shoulder of Una's ensemble. "Your dress is beautiful. The dark green is perfect with the coloring of your hair and eyes."

The compliment brought both joy and sadness. Relenting, she'd remodeled her scruffy wedding dress, dying the fabric with water in which she'd steeped coffee grounds and alfalfa. Had the dress caught Ryker's attention—the same dress she'd worn when proclaiming her love to another man? But surely the frock had taken on new meaning. The dress had been down the river and over the mill, like her own life, twisted and reshaped beyond what either had once been. They were both made of malleable and resilient fabric.

"I've seen your wedding picture, I know this dress meant a lot to you then, and by your wistful expression you are still clinging to the past. Life is for the living, Una. The heart is big enough to love many people, for many reasons. When my son was born, I didn't think I could love anyone as much as I love Jordie, but I do. I adore little Jedidiah in a special way only a parent can."

"Take a breath, dear Kate. If I wasn't trying to move on, I wouldn't be here tonight. But moving on with Ryker feels like wandering through the twisted footpaths in Break Heart Canyon. There is no way to tell what's waiting around the next wall of rock. Or if

I'll ever get out at all and end up alone, lost forever."

"Despite his original reason for coming here, he seems a man of good intentions. And as far as getting lost in Break Heart Canyon, with the heart of an explorer and the courage of a soldier, he won't let either one of you get lost."

"Aye," Una gave a chuckle, "He's a ramstoorie, to be sure—rough and ready," she translated at Kate's questioning expression.

"All right then. Enjoy your evening out. They're rare enough."

Una wanted to do just that, but more concerns worried her mind. "Kate, the men are up to something else tonight besides eating and drinking. Ryker's been conferring with Mr. Jim these last few days. Conversations which cease when I appear. They've been acting like wee lads up to mischief. Which brings me to wondering exactly where is Mr. Jim."

"I've not seen him, but the night is young."

"Not so young when I must be up at dawn or suffer a terrible rendition of a donkey duet."

"I don't know how you keep going out there on your own."

"First of all, I'm not on my own. I've got honey bees, a barn full of sweet animals, plus all the creatures Mother Nature sees fit to send my way. Second of all, what else would I be doin'?

"There's comfort in my spinning, and a good days work out of doors is freedom itself. I'd not do well like you and Jordie, confined to four walls in a bank or schoolhouse."

"Quite the pretty speech, and I grant you, your lifestyle brings roses to your cheeks, but you are well aware of what I mean. Sharing your love—"

Midsentence, Una gave Kate a quick hug, stopping the familiar good-hearted lecture regarding her solitary life. "You are the best friend I've ever had, and I'm blessed you worry over me, but can we please speak of another matter?"

Kate laughed and nodded, and just in time as Jordie and Ryker returned to their side.

As he approached, Ryker's gaze travelled the length of her from top to bottom and back up again. "For the prettiest lady here." He handed her a cup of punch in the fanciest cut crystal she'd ever seen.

"Thank you." Heat prickled her cheeks. She took a sip, and turned her gaze aside to escape his scrutiny and hide how much his compliment meant to her.

Too soon, the enjoyable ripple of pleasure was replaced by a sinking feeling. Seeming to have noticed their presence, Boss Pritchard broke free of his adoring group, and with a purposeful stride, his face contorted into a most unfriendly expression, he headed their way. Trailing in his wake, were several men including Ryker's employer, Mr. Cockrell.

"I'm afraid of that man and his underlings." Una whispered. "They have dark souls."

"Like I said, the exact reason why we're here. To show them, scared or not, we aren't going to give in to their bullying tactics. Besides, in a few minutes Mr. Pritchard will have other concerns."

"What's that supposed to be meanin'."

"Just a little taste of the mayhem he's been causing. Nothing serious, a bit of well-deserved embarrassment to disrupt his special day and to take him down a peg or two."

As if on cue, Pritchard's main man, the one they'd encountered at the front door, hurried across the room interrupting their host's forward momentum. Two men carrying satchels marched behind the ranch hand. They wore suits and grim expressions.

"They got badges, boss. I couldn't stop 'em."

"What's all this about then?" Chest puffed out, hands on his hips, Pritchard confronted the intruders.

"You're under arrest for illegal distillation and bootlegging of alcoholic liquor."

"This is preposterous."

"Don't make a fuss, come along quiet. We saw the still, we got you dead to rights."

"If there is a distillery on my property, somebody obviously planted the apparatus. I buy my liquor in town. I'm rich, I don't need to make the sour mash rotgut you call moonshine."

"Facts is facts. You need to come with us. Mr. Silas Pritchard, you're under arrest."

"Well, here's a new fact for you." Boss Pritchard withdrew a large ornate handgun from inside his frock coat. "This gun and my men say I'm not guilty of the trumped-up charges you're throwing around." In the soft glow of the chandelier, the weapon's pearl handle gleamed and the silver barrel shone brightly enough to be seen across the room.

As a man stepped up behind the revenuers, she heard Ryker inhale sharply. The unknown person's visage reminding her of...Mr. Jim. How was this possible? Dressed as well or better than anyone present, the man's grey hair was trimmed and swept back highlighting his clean-shaven noble face.

She squinted—not believing her eyes. But it was

Mr. Jim, or at least the man who had been lurking beneath the rough exterior. He stood tall, a commanding figure. The revenuers and Boss Pritchard were momentarily forgotten as all eyes turned toward her friend.

"You can arrest him for murder too." At Mr. Jim's words, the silent room came alive, and all hell broke loose.

The revenuers backed up a few steps. Mr. Cockrell scurried over to hide behind Ryker. Along with Una, Kate, and Jordie they formed a solitary knot in the sea of onlookers.

Waving his pistol, keeping everyone at bay, Pritchard went on the defense, directing his conversation toward Mr. Jim. "Well, if it isn't Mr. James Henry Merriman. You're back I see, and no doubt behind this travesty of false charges. And still singing the same old song of revenge and retribution."

"I've been around the whole time, watching you run roughshod over the county. And a song based on truth never goes out of fashion."

The light of understanding crossed Pritchard's face. "You sneaky old dog. You've been nosing around the town like a down and out drifter, while living the high life up on the hill."

"Life hasn't been particularly high since you murdered my wife and those miners on Christmas Eve two years ago."

"You've no proof I or my men were anywhere near that mine when the explosion and cave-in occurred."

Jim retrieved a pistol from his coat pocket. "I believe this is yours." The weapon matched the fancy one Pritchard held. Jim's bore the letter P engraved on the ivory handle. Pritchard's gun showed the letter S.

"Silas Pritchard, you killed those people in the hopes of driving me off my land. Just like you've been harassing Mrs. MacLaren and anybody else who gets in your way. I found this clutched in the hand of my mortally wounded employee who was outside when the blast went off. He named you and your boys as the villains. And only someone on the scene would know an explosion had caused the mine to collapse.

"I've been waiting a long time to catch you flashing your cherished pistol in public. I figured tonight your ego would get the better of you, and with two years having passed, you'd take the chance you were finally safe to do so."

"The weapon you're holding could belong to anybody, initialed or not."

"The gunsmith who made them swears they belong to you. His mark is right here, and I'm betting there is a similar mark on the one you're holding."

Pritchard glanced from side to side as if assessing the best path for a quick exit.

"The witness also named Curly Joe and Bearcat as being there on that day of death." The cowhands eased away from their boss. "You're all guilty of murder."

"So you've got a pistol you could have found anywhere and the word of a dead man. You still can't prove I was there."

"The miner I mentioned lived three days. Long enough to sign a written statement, witnessed and validated by several people. At my bidding, they've kept secret about what they knew regarding that dastardly day."

Pritchard surveyed the crowd as if trying to

determine who might have been playing him false all this time. "If these witnesses know what's good for them, they'll keep quiet. And you men better do the same."

"I reckon Curly Joe and Bearcat might want to clear their consciences to save their own necks from a rope. Including fessing up to the *accident* which took the life of Hamish MacLaren." The two men stepped back another few paces extricating themselves farther from the man they once called boss.

Firing the revolver, which had sealed his fate, Pritchard continued to blast away and made a break for the side door. As the bullets came too close for comfort, Ryker shoved Mr. Cockrell aside, saving the man's life in exchange for a new wound in his previously injured shoulder. "Dang, this is never going to heal."

Quick on the heels of Mr. Pritchard, the revenuers disappeared though the fancy double doors and into the night. A scuffle ensued in the darkness out on the well-manicured lawn.

****

Una helped Ryker out of his jacket. Ripping off a piece of her dress, she pressed the fabric to his injury.

Mr. Jim hurried over to join them. "Sorry for the collateral damage. Pain and suffering follow that man like an evil shadow."

"Barely grazed me. I've had worse," Ryker reassured. "When you agreed to get the moonshiners to set up my revenuers' scheme, I knew you had a plan of your own, but this beats all."

"Cletus and the boys enjoyed the ruse as much as you. And I didn't think you'd mind sharing the spotlight for a good cause."

"Nope. It sheds light on things we talked of before."

Mr. Cockrell staggered over, one hand to his chest as if making sure his heart continued to beat, "Good gracious, you saved my life, Landry. Does this happen often out West?"

"It's not unheard of." The minor wound had nearly stopped bleeding, and with the pad made of Una's dress held in place by his shirt, Ryker replaced his jacket.

"Consider your account paid in full," his ex-employer offered, the paleness of his complexion still noticeable.

"Well, I should think so." Una knew she should hold her tongue, but the man rubbed her the wrong way and she blamed him for Ryker being shot. "You might even be owin' him a good bit of change." Her remark drew murmurs of agreement and a few hoots from those gathered around. At Ryker's sputtering laugh, she was glad she'd spoken up.

****

After what had transpired, the party ended in haste. The confused guests either took their leave in silent wonder, or in lively discussion at the revelations heard tonight.

Mr. Jim's departure was delayed with further questioning by the Federal agents. Appearing a bit peely-wally after his near-death experience, Mr. Cockrell hitched a ride with Kate and Jordie back to Cañon City and civilization.

"Whiskey sure pulled one over on us." Ryker handed Una up into her jaunty pink carriage, then he settled onto the seat at her side. "And he sure had his reasons."

"I've known Mr. Jim longer than you, yet you seem to be more acquainted with his story."

"Sitting in the dark around a campfire at night, men tend to share talk they might not otherwise discuss during the light of day."

"Well, the hens have flown the coop, for heaven's sake, tell me everything. All I know is Mr. Jim has now revealed himself as the man on the hill, and he tragically lost his wife. More heartbreak in Break Heart Canyon.

"That's pretty much the gist of it. When his wife died, he went mad with grief, becoming a complete recluse, and the scruffy unrecognizable Whiskey Jim was born. But his need for justice lived on. As long as the town believed the owner remained housebound, his vagabond disguise allowed him to manage his property while he waited for Pritchard to show his hand.

"He considered fessing up a time or two, but when the unseen man on the hill became a living legend shrouded in mystery, Jim felt obligated to keep up the ruse."

"But Mr. Jim… All this time… He fooled me so easily. I feel quite betrayed. And I'll miss the kind man I'd befriended."

"The man we first knew still exists. Whiskey did what he had to do in order to survive his loss, you can understand such pain firsthand. And he needed the anonymity in order to bring Pritchard to justice. His necessary deception and the cause for which he fought didn't lessen his concern for your needs and safety. He holds you dear to his heart."

"Aye, that's true enough. He was the only one who believed Hamish's death wasn't an accident. I thank him for gaining justice for me too. Did he tell you what happened at the silver mine, and how Pritchard was involved?"

Ryker nodded. "I've patched together bits and pieces from our talks. Apparently, the tragedy occurred on the day before Christmas. The miners insisted on working because they got double-time wages. At noon, Jim's wife took them special treats she'd baked along with the news they were all to go home to their families and still expect to get a full day's pay.

"Jim's witness had been stationed at the mine entrance. Becoming bored he went on a short walkabout. That's when Jim's wife arrived unseen and stepped inside. When the guard returned, he caught Pritchard and his men up to no good.

"Confronting the men got him shot for his trouble. He didn't die from the explosion, but from a bullet wound when he wrenched the pistol from Pritchard's hand."

"So he lived three days because he hadn't been buried in the mine."

"Correct. Fearing the gun shot would bring the other miners out, and the TNT already having been placed, Pritchard and the men detonated the explosives, then hightailed it before they could recover the pistol.

"No one knew Mrs. Merriman was present. When the blast went off, she was thrown clear, but fatally wounded."

"Oh, poor Mr. Jim. A time or two, I've caught an expression in his eyes giving away the fact his heart was broken. But why wait so long to bring Boss Pritchard to justice?"

"Worried the document might not be enough, he

laid low putting Pritchard off his guard. A reasonable plan. Then when this occasion arose for his enemy to flaunt the matching pistol in public with the Federal Agents there to seal the deal, my rather innocent ploy became an opportunity for initiating his long-awaited showdown."

"It's all quite fantastic." Una mulled over all she'd learned tonight.

"Around here, how could you expect less?"

She couldn't disagree with him there. "Now that all has been revealed, I hope Mr. Jim finds comfort, and the town folk will continue to treat him kindly for the deception."

As they halted in front of Una's cabin, The Countess gave a welcoming heehaw. Ryker handed Una down. Then despite his minor wound, and without hesitation, he unhitched Wallace and put up the rig as if he'd gone through the motions a hundred times. His familiarity of her little world was a comfort. Then a stab of loneliness struck deep.

"From now on, I should be safe from those wretched cattlemen, so there's no need for you to be remainin' here with me."

"There's other reasons I'd like to stay."

"Such as…."

Stepping closer, Ryker grasped her upper arms and gave her a kiss, and a precious moment in time never to be forgotten. He fed the hunger waiting within her all these years, and weak-kneed, she wrapped her arms around him and held on tight.

"Is kissing me your only reason, then?" she asked as they broke apart to catch their breath.

"Let's say kissing is a good place to start until I can

show you more."

The rush of love buzzing through her brain nearly obscured his words as she envisioned what showing her more might entail. Then she pointed out the hard truth. "If you're no longer my man for hire, you living here would be unseemly."

"Yes, very much so. I guess we'd better get married."

Chapter Twenty-One

Without a moment's hesitation, Una accepted Ryker's proposal. And now, three week later, as the ceremony joining them together forever was about to begin, her heart felt ready to burst with joy.

Mr. Jim had insisted the wedding take place at his home-on-the-hill, beneath the beautiful arbor now decorated with streamers and the last of the summer flowers.

High-stepping as if she realized this was a special occasion, The Countess, a profusion of daisies woven into her mane, drew the bright pink cart to the matrimonial destination. MacTavish sat on the seat beside Una, a jaunty plaid scarf tied around his neck. Tongue lolling, he dog-grinned up at her as if to say riding rather than walking was much to his liking.

"Don't be growing accustomed to such luxury, you scruffy hound. It's only for one glorious day." He whined then yipped, and she gave him a hug.

Brushing the stray dog hairs from the beautiful fabric of her dress, Una recalled how worried she'd been about what to wear for her wedding. But Kate had come to her rescue by secretly commandeering the mothers of the school children. Grateful for the woolen caps Una had knit for their children last Christmas, the moms were more than happy to pitch in. Their combined skills had created an ethereal ivory gown for

Una, and their kindness and generosity touched her deeply.

Excited to see the fruits of their labor, the women and their husbands had been invited to the ceremony. And she'd also been informed the moonshiners might be observing from the nearby trees.

Then Mr. Jim added the crowning touch by offering for Ryker to purchase, at an amazingly good price, a ring for her that had been in the Merriman family for generations. How proudly she would wear the symbol of their love.

As the cart crested a small hill, the sun dipped lower turning the few clouds in the sky to blazing pink and startling blue. And framed by such beauty, before her lay the future she could hardly wait to begin

Kate, Jordie, and Mr. Jim stood with the preacher under the latticed wooden timbers. But where was Ryker? He should have been standing there as well.

Her heart skipped a beat, but not in a good way. Had his lifetime of adventuring gotten the better of him, sending him packing at the last minute?

Jordie stepped up and reached for The Countess's bridal bringing the little carriage to a halt. Kate hurried forward to hand her the lovely bouquet she'd arranged.

"Where is he?" Una whispered.

"Have faith. He's nearby."

"We're going to be late." Ryker's voice rang out from the other side of the arbor. He sounded distraught. Then she heard Wallace making an even more disgruntled sound. The Countess fidgeted and answered his call.

Una now understood the delay. Having her furry friends attend the ceremony had been her idea, but regardless of how joyous the reason, the two donkeys did not do well when separated.

Just when she thought she couldn't stand the suspense a moment longer, Ryker stepped out from behind the wooden trellis.

Dressed in what was most certainly evening attire on loan from Mr. Jim, Ryker filled out the black suit and white shirt as if it were tailor made just for him. His hair was tied back at the nape of his neck, and clean shaven and smiling, he'd never appeared more handsome. He could take the place of any Scottish storybook hero she'd read about as a child.

When Ryker tugged on the lead gripped tightly in his left hand, Wallace appeared. Sporting a large bowtie, with a seen-better-days top hat anchored on his head, he danced and bucked with joy, sending a wave of mirth through all gathered together today.

At the sound of laughter, Wallace grew completely rambunctious. Ryker unhooked the lead, and not stopping for anyone or anything, the gelding sideswiped Ryker and sprinted toward the *woman* he loved—The Countess.

The two donkeys nuzzled one another, but Una's gaze was riveted on Ryker. Righting himself and straightening his apparel, he advanced, and the love in his eyes allayed her fears for today and all the days to come.

With the brightest of smiles, he hurried to her side, and she gained her feet as he reached to hand her down from the cart. Just then, her nemesis the rogue fox, streaked beneath the carriage wheels and between the legs of The Countess. Startled by the confusion the donkey reared upsetting the cart. In hot pursuit,

MacTavish dove off the seat and Wallace heehawed encouragingly.

Una yelped in surprise, and with lace and petticoats flying she was thrust into Ryker's waiting arms. He caught her with ease and held her close. Cozened like a child against his broad chest, she never felt so safe— safe and in love—now and forever.

Her friends, and even the preacher, broke into laughter. The merriment rose another octave as ever impetuous and not one to worry about a little thing like breaking the rules, Ryker spun around with her still in his arms, and the ceremony began with a kiss rather than ending with one.

Epilogue

Brushing the sleep from her eyes, Una greeted the morning with a happy murmur as she peered over the soft warm mountain of covers.

Filled with the impetuous and naïve bravado of those madly in love, she and Ryker had dared one another to spend their first night as husband and wife in the Spirit Cave. Stretching sideways, she reached for him. He wasn't there.

Bolting upright, she glanced around. Had their night of loving been but a glorious dream? Her wedding dress lay beside the basket of goodies they'd brought for a midnight snack, and the ring on her finger reassured her the wedding had been real.

After the sumptuous feast prepared by their friends, and following the goodbyes and good wishes, she and Ryker had made wild and passionate love in her cabin. An experience beyond her imagining. Then deciding they must find their heart songs in the Spirit Cave, they created a cozy nest and made love there too—a much slower and tender joining of body and soul.

But where had he gone?

Easing from beneath the covers, she ran her hands through her tangle of hair, and slipped into a light chemise. Wrapped in her plaid shawl and a growing eagerness to be once again in Ryker's arms, she peeked out of the cave. MacTavish, still refusing to come inside waited for her, and together they made their way into the bright light of day.

Ryker stood beside Strawberry Creek, the morning light dancing and sparkling off the rushing water. Coming up behind him, she wrapped her arms around his waist and nestled one cheek against his strong broad back—he was humming a tune. The melody was familiar, she'd heard the same one last night. Humming an octave higher, she joined him in a slightly off-key duet.

He turned to face her. "You heard it too."

She nodded. "Our heart-song is the same."

"How could it not be."

"Are you happy here? Will the farm and the canyon be enough for you?" The question came out before she weighed the ramifications his answer might hold.

"You will be enough for me. And I feel as if I've searched the world over to find this exact spot."

"And I feel you were sent to mend my heart and make this a happy place once again."

"Well, thank goodness we have all those pesky details resolved," he jested. "Here. I was washing this off in the stream. I meant to give it to you yesterday, but never found the right time." He placed an object in her hands she hadn't noticed he held.

"But how…"

"The day you pawned the stone, I was in town. Even from afar, your indecision and sacrifice were obvious."

"I was so sad when I learned my treasure had been sold. Oh, thank you, Ryker, thank you." What a thoughtful wedding gift from her new husband, and having the geode back also felt like Hamish was giving his blessing as to how thing had turned out "This beautiful stone means more to me now than ever."

"And you mean more to me than you will ever know."

"Then you must tell me every night."

"I promise—in word and deed."

Hands overlapping, they held tight to the precious stone.

Splashing through Strawberry Creek, MacTavish loped over to them, stopped, and shook, showering them from head to toe with ice-cold water.

"From now on," Ryker gasped, "there will be no more heartbreak in Break Heart canyon."

Una smiled and wiped the water from her face. "Only love and laughter."

Author's Note

The Bone Wars, also known as the Great Dinosaur Rush, was a period of intense and ruthlessly competitive fossil hunting and discovery during the Gilded Age of American history. Marked by a heated rivalry between Edward Drinker Cope and Othniel Charles Marsh, the treachery and battles began in 1877 and ended in 1892.

The total solar eclipse of July 1878 traveled through British Columbia, along the spine of the Rocky Mountains and directly over the state of Colorado. When newspapers across the country made the eclipse headline news, the phenomenon sparked interest in science for everyday people. Asaph Hall, who had recently discovered the Martian moons, was in Colorado, as was Maria Mitchell, leading an all-female expedition to show the world what women astronomers could do.

Regarding giants once inhabiting the Earth. Is my ancient chief character purely fantasy? Around the Grand Canyon, and in Lovelock, Nevada, Provo, Utah, and the Missouri Ozarks stories and legends abound supporting the fact such beings existed. Several museums are reported to house giant skeletal remains, but the artifacts are not on display.

A word about the author…

Gini Rifkin lives on a little patch of land where she takes in abandoned farm animals. When not reading or chasing the fur babies, she's learning to spin goat hair and is weaving more than her next story. Her award-winning books include the Medieval, Victorian, Old West, and contemporary time periods. Your next adventure awaits.

http://ginirifkin.blogspot.com

Gini is winner of The Beverley Award, the Maple Leaf Award, Best Romantic Thriller, Paranormal Guild Reviewer's Choice Award, Reader's Choice Award, and Publisher's Pick.

Other books by Gini…

Fatal Recall
Undercover Outlaw
Trapper's Moon
Cowboys, Cattle, and Cutthroats
Solace: Fae Warriors Book 1
Bliss: Fae Warriors Book 2
Portence: Fae Warriors Book 3
A Cowboy's Fate
Special Delivery
Waiting for Caleb: Australia Burns
Victorian Dream
Lady Gallant
Iron Heart
The Dragon and The Rose